SUICIDE MISSION

A STAR NATION IN PERIL
BOOK 2

SKYLER RAMIREZ

The characters and events portrayed in this book are fictitious. Any similarity to real persons, living or dead, is coincidental and not intended by the author.

eBook ISBN: 978-1-964457-07-9

Paperback ISBN: 978-1-964457-57-4

Printed in the United States of America

Published by Persephone Entertainment Inc.

Texas, USA

Don't ever miss a new release!

Sign up now for Skyler's newsletter and get access to new release updates, free content, and great deals.

Just go to www.skylerramirez.com/join-the-club

CONTENTS

PROLOGUE

She stopped running and leaned back hard against the rough brick wall, heaving great gasping breaths and trying desperately to collect her thoughts. The wall was rough and sharp through her thin, sweat-soaked, torn shirt, but the coolness of the brick felt good against her skin in the warmth of the summer night.

She slowed her breathing as best she could and strained to listen. The barking of the dogs had stopped. Did that mean they had lost her scent in the city's morass? Or had their handlers quieted them so as not to alert her of their close approach?

It almost didn't matter. She'd been running for so long already that she needed a brief respite, or she was likely to make a mistake. But now, images of a different blood-spattered alley filled her thoughts; she hadn't had time to process what had happened there, was it less than half an hour before?

A sound at the open end of the alley ripped her out of her own head and back into the moment. It had been a small noise like a foot lightly scuffing the pavement, but it portended far bigger and more dangerous things.

She glanced quickly around the dumpster that shielded her from view deep in the narrow space and resisted the urge to swear out loud. She *hadn't* lost them. And as they moved down the alley toward her, assault rifles extended on their slings and scanning back and forth, she knew the end had come.

She pulled out the only weapon left to her. Guns ran out of ammunition, even modern railguns that required only a few grams of metal and could store hundreds of shots before running dry. But a knife never ran out. It was one of the many reasons she'd always preferred her blade over a gun in so many situations.

This was *not* one of them.

But there was nothing to be done about it. The alley was closed off by a tall fence behind her, and there was no way she could scale that in plain view of her pursuers before they riddled her with dozens of rounds. She might as well go out fighting then, even if the outcome would be the same.

Heather Kilgore took a deep breath, tightened her grip on the knife's hilt, made slick with her sweat, and stepped calmly out from behind the dumpster and toward her death.

ONE
FATEFUL ORDERS
HEATHER KILGORE

F*ive Weeks Earlier*

'You, Agent Kilgore, will kill the Koratan president's wife and daughter. That will send the message our King intends. This mission *cannot* fail.'

Those words, spoken to Heather Kilgore just one week before, haunted her dreams. Every time she closed her eyes, she heard them echoing inside her head. Everywhere she went, out of the corner of her eye, she saw the dour gaze of her boss, head of the Order of the King's Cross, as he delivered the death sentence to two people none of them had ever met from light years away.

She still hadn't even left Hudson to follow the orders. She kept telling herself that it was so she could finalize the prep work that was so vital to a mission deep within enemy lines. But, in her heart, she knew she was stalling.

As an agent of the King's Cross, Heather Kilgore had many times done things she wasn't proud of. Once, she'd killed a woman because she'd threatened to blackmail a member of the royal family. Another time, she'd murdered the adolescent son of a duke because his father had planned a coup against the King, and the monarch was worried the son would carry on his elder's work—that had been the mission that had destroyed her friendship with Tabitha Lowry. Then, just a few weeks ago, she'd sunk a knife into Tabitha and used the same knife to end the life of the only man she'd ever loved.

So, undertaking a mission on which she had mixed feelings was nothing new to her. But this…

It would be one thing to kill the Koratan president, Francisco Ignacio Juarez, in retaliation for his ordering an invasion of Hudson and the Harper Line that would have surely started a full-scale war between Prometheus and Koratas. After all, no one would really blame King Charles for taking revenge on his Koratan counterpart for the attempted attack—the attack that had only failed because Heather had helped expose it in time to rally Second Fleet to be waiting at Hudson when the Koratan fleet arrived—but Heather's orders weren't to go after Ignacio Juarez.

In her implant, she had two pictures. One was of a woman in her forties with a regal bearing who still managed to look young and innocent, though Heather couldn't pinpoint exactly what it was in the photo that gave her that impression. The other…the other was of a little girl, just nine years old and full of life. Heather couldn't even look at that one for more than the few seconds it had taken her to memorize the little girl's face.

But, ultimately, no matter how distasteful the mission, she had her orders, and no member of the King's Cross would ever ignore or disobey an order from their sovereign—she kept telling herself that despite Tabitha's recent betrayal. So, a week after receiving her orders, Heather finally boarded a starliner headed into Koratan territory, the fake passport on her implant granting her passage to her first stop on her long journey to kill a wife and daughter.

TWO
A TEAM EFFORT
SPARROW

Katarina was very annoyed. The target wasn't where he was supposed to be, which wasn't possible. The man was a creature of habit. Every weekday at exactly two p.m., he went to the coffee shop on the corner of Calle Chavez and Calle Heraldo—every day without deviation.

Except today. Today the man had instead decided to go out to early afternoon drinks with some colleagues—one of them was having a birthday, apparently—which completely messed up Katarina's plan!

Relajate, Trina told her. *Things don't always go according to plan, chica. Sometimes you have to improvise.*

Katarina ignored her. Trina was always saying useless things like that—always telling her to relax—but it was Katarina's plans that kept them all alive. Still…

She sighed and stood up from the seat in the coffee shop and went outside into the bright afternoon Koratas sun, shielding her eyes and squinting. She hated the sunlight and far preferred the dimmer lights of the inside world, but there was nothing for it now; the target wasn't where he was supposed to be!

I can handle this! Let me drive now, chica, Trina insisted, but Katarina kept ignoring her. Maybe if she ignored her long enough, she'd go away.

No such luck. Halfway down the block, Katarina had to face facts: her plan was a no-go, and she wasn't the best at improvising. She didn't want to give up control—she could practically feel Trina's giddiness at the inevitable surrender—but there was nothing else she could do right now.

Fine! she thought at Trina and stopped at a street vendor selling cheap t-shirts and hats. She stood in front of a small mirror taped to a rack of hats and pulled one on at random, grimacing as she did so but triggering a special routine in her implant that activated another implant—different from the ones most people had in their heads—nearer to her scalp and extending down near her ocular nerves.

A minute later, she took off the hat and looked in the mirror. Gone were Katarina's brown locks and her plain brown eyes. Looking back now in the mirror were the crazy blue hair and bright green eyes of Trina.

Gracias! Trina called happily. *I was getting so bored, you have no idea, chica. Now, let's go get this hombre.*

Trina paid for the hat—she didn't really like it, but she knew Katarina hated the way hats looked on them, so she was willing to wear it just to annoy the other woman—and started walking down the street toward the bar that her implant and the drones overhead told her the target was inside.

En route, she passed in front of the target's place of work, making sure she kept the hat pulled low and her eyes straight ahead as she did so. No one there knew her, of course, but it paid to be careful anyway. Even Trina acknowledged that, though she knew that Katarina would have probably gone two blocks out of her way just to be extra careful. But Katarina was boring, and Trina was anxious to get to the next part.

A few minutes later, she arrived at the bar and slipped inside, moving quickly through the door after opening it only a crack; she didn't want to be caught outlined in the sunlight from outside, at least not until she got the lay of the place.

Once inside, she quickly moved to sit in a small booth, ignoring the bartender's glance and letting her eyes adjust to the dimly lit space. It only took her a moment to spot the target, and she watched him for a couple of minutes. He was young, older than her, but still only 28, and he had the pale skin and blond hair so common to people from his star nation. On Koratas, which was populated mostly by those of Latino descent, it made him stand out.

He was talking and laughing with two co-workers, a male and a female. From the way he kept glancing at the woman, he had a crush on her, but the way she held onto the other man's arm told the sad story of love unrequited.

Too bad. Everyone should experience at least a little love before they die.

Which gave Trina an idea. None of the group at the bar had seen her yet, so she made sure the hat was still pulled down tightly on her head and triggered her special implant again. She didn't have a mirror, but she knew that her blue hair was slowly turning red—not like a natural redhead, but more of a bottle-dyed and bold red that was popular these days with Koratan young women. Her eyes were also changing from green to blue, though that happened almost instantaneously.

Her implant pinged her that the transformation was done, and Victoria yawned.

Trina, por que—why? I was resting. A garota needs her beauty sleep. Why did you wake me?

Focus, Victoria! Katarina snapped. It was good of her to speak up; Trina had already lost interest. *The target is right over there. You need to get him out of the bar,* Katarina finished.

But não quero—I don't want to, garota, I'm...hey, he's cute! Without further argument, Victoria stood up from the table, taking off the hat to let her red hair fall loose and stretching languidly. She caught a few of the men in the bar watching her do it and she winked at one of them.

Focus, Victoria. The target! Katarina chided, and Victoria stuck out her lower lip in a pout.

Still, she started walking across the bar, wishing she had her high heels to clack on the faux wood floor—stupid Katarina had insisted they wear running shoes; the moça had no sense of style. But still, Victoria was good at her job, and she sashayed her hips as she walked and made sure to catch the target's eye but then quickly looked away as if she hadn't seen him and was oblivious to him watching her the entire way.

Funny enough, the woman he was with threw Victoria a dirty look even though her boyfriend didn't look Victoria's way even once. Maybe she actually was sweet on the target, at least enough to be jealous of his attention being diverted to another woman.

"Tequila shot," Victoria said as she arrived at the bar right next to the target.

The bartender nodded and started pouring, and Victoria cocked out a hip as if she were getting comfortable. Her hip bumped the target's thigh—she was a lot shorter than him—and he turned and regarded her in surprise.

"Perdoe-me," she said in her native Portuguese with a coy smile as the bartender handed her the shot. Holding the target's startled gaze, she knocked back the tequila and then licked her lips. He watched every move she made, being painfully obvious about it.

"Uh, it's OK, Miss..."

"Victoria," she said, holding out her free hand as she put

the shot glass, upside down, on the bar in front of her and motioned for another. "And you are?"

He told her his name, though she already knew it, and she repeated it in an overemphasized version of her accent that she knew drove most men a little bit crazy. The way his eyes widened at hearing her say it, she knew it was working on him.

"Do you come here often?" he asked next, and she fought the urge to roll her eyes at the least creative pickup line in the history of the galaxy. *Really, Trina,* she thought. *He's cute, but you woke me up for this?*

But she answered anyway, and she kept chatting with him as she downed a second, then a third shot of tequila. As Victoria drank each shot, she saw the man's eyes start to get more hopeful—he had no way of knowing how good her implant was at deadening the alcohol's effect. For the third shot, she had him drink one as well, his two friends forgotten behind him. And though he cast a few furtive glances back at his female friend a time or two, Victoria was always able to bring his hungry gaze back to her.

It was way too easy.

When she invited him back to her place, he accepted eagerly, even though it was still only the afternoon. She claimed to live just three blocks away, within easy walking distance. He bid a hasty farewell to his friends, ignoring or not catching the flash of anger in the other woman's eyes, and followed Victoria out the bar door, practically bouncing with excitement. Her biggest regret was leaving behind the hat; it might not have been Trina's style—and heaven forbid the stodgy Katarina ever be caught in a hat—but Victoria liked the way it looked on her. Still, the mission had to come first.

The target followed Victoria down Calle Chavez, grinning dumbly the entire time and chatting her up like he thought he might lose her if he didn't keep her talking. Victoria played the game, laughing at his not-funny jokes and oohing and aahing at the inventive descriptions of his oh-so-boring government job.

She kept stringing him along all the way up until two blocks later, when they passed the narrow alleyway Katarina had tagged on their implant as a good spot based on a variety of boring metrics she tried to explain to Victoria until Trina shushed her out of habit.

She slowed down as they neared the alley, and eventually, the man looked over at her. She saw his sudden confusion.

"Hey, wasn't your hair red?" he asked, and then he met her eyes and his widened.

For a second, he looked like he might open his mouth to yell, but Lola put her left hand over his mouth and shoved him roughly into the alley. There, without any hesitation, she slammed the edge of her other hand right into his windpipe, crushing it and cutting off any noise he may have made.

He slumped to the ground, falling amongst several bags of garbage from an adjacent restaurant. Lola looked down at him, her gray eyes cold and unfeeling as he grasped for breath and clutched at his neck with both hands, but to no avail. Without immediate medical attention, he was already dead.

She kept watching while, in her peripheral vision, she verified that no one else was close enough to have seen her pull the man into the alley, and no one passing on the other side of the street even glanced their way. It was still early afternoon, and most people were still at work.

The man finally stopped gasping and struggling and lay still with a final rattling exhale, and Lola smiled; that was her favorite part, watching the life go out of the body. She reached up and stroked her stark white hair almost lovingly as she studied the corpse at her feet, ignoring Katarina's shudder and Victoria's stifled gasp as she did so. Reaching down, Lola pulled the ID badge out of the dead man's pocket and tossed it onto his stomach, where it would be the first thing anyone who found him would see.

She didn't bother dragging him deeper into the alley or even putting any of the trash bags over him. They wanted him to be found; it would send the proper message. The ID badge had his smiling picture on it, just above his name—which wasn't important—and below his employer's name—which was supremely important. In fact, his employer was the only reason he had to die. Two weeks ago, they'd killed a spy from her nation operating inside theirs, so retaliation was necessary, even vital, to maintain the balance of power.

Lola smiled again as she reread the words on the top of the now dead target's ID badge: 'The Federated Systems of Prometheus'. Yes, the Promethean embassy would be quite upset when they found the body of one of their low-level diplomats, but it would send the right message:

Don't mess with the Koratan Confederacy.

E 'fatto, Lola said to the others in her native Italian—'it's finished'. Then she turned and started walking out of the alley.

A few minutes later, as she walked along the streets in a way that would have appeared aimless to anyone watching, her implant pinged.

"Gorrión"—Sparrow—"Is it done?" an older woman's voice asked in her head, the implant converting the electronic message into a passable approximation of the real woman's voice.

"Sí, Nido," she replied simply, also via her implant.

"Good. Come back to base. We have your next mission."

Ooh, another mission, how exciting! I can't wait to start planning, Katarina exulted.

Silencio, aburrida, Trina replied snidely. Those two were always at each other's throats, and only Trina's usually short attention span kept the fights from spiraling out of control.

I hope it's another man; that was fun, though maybe next time we don't have to kill him so quickly, Victoria said with a yawn, already halfway back to sleep.

Lola said nothing; she rarely did unless absolutely necessary.

Sparrow ignored them all as best she could. "I'm on my way, Nido," she replied, taking back control. "Ten minutes." By the time the call ended, she was already a block further toward the base and her hair was back to its natural black and her eyes their natural hazel. She tried to never let Nido—Nest—see her any other way—no use advertising the others who lived in her head with her. She liked Nido—the woman was a good boss—and it would be a shame for Lola to have to kill her if she ever figured out Sparrow's secret.

After all, they didn't let insane people be members of the Koratan Confederate Guard, and if there was perhaps only one thing that Katarina, Trina, Victoria, and Lola could all agree on, it was that they loved their job.

THREE
A SPARROW'S NEST
SPARROW

Sparrow grunted in pain and frustration as the knife bit into her cheek. She'd seen the attack coming but had been an instant too slow in either blocking or dodging the blade and could now feel the warmth of blood running down her face.

Still, she knew that to stop, even for the barest instant, to check or nurse her wound would be to invite far worse. So, she lashed out with one foot, catching her attacker in the solar plexus even as the knife was finishing its swing and before her assailant could bring it back around to defend or attack again.

The result was a satisfying grunt from the larger woman, followed by another as Sparrow's hand lashed outward and upward into the soft cartilage of her nose, causing her to bleed as badly as Sparrow and almost ending the fight as her eyes filled with water. But the other woman was still too fast for Sparrow to land the killing blow, springing back and out of her short arms' length range, buying herself just enough time to get back into a defensive stance after wiping the involuntary tears.

Sparrow feinted toward the older woman but then moved back quickly when her reaction was no slower than normal for the pain of her broken nose. Silently, she swore at the delay, letting her opponent get a chance to recover, but it also gave her a moment to collect herself.

Let me take her, per favore, Lola said, her voice somehow eager but still cold.

The older woman feinted a kick, and a distracted Sparrow —who had to pause a moment to fight against Lola's attempts to seize control—bit on it a little too quickly, blocking low and missing the hard fist that slammed into the side of her head, knocking her to the floor and out of the fight.

Sparrow jerked awake a few seconds later as her opponent held smelling salts under her nose, flailing and kicking in the moment of disorientation but then settling down as she recognized the face peering down at her.

"Estás mejorando gorrioncita," the woman said with a wry smile. 'You're getting better, little Sparrow.'

She might have taken offense at the 'little' part, but Sparrow was the name by which the woman knew her, just as she knew the older woman only as 'Nido'—Nest.

"You got me again," Sparrow gasped once she'd caught her breath, and Nest helped her up from the thin mat, which was the sparring area's one and only concession to safety. Even the blades they fought with were real, though Nido had managed to knock hers from her grasp less than a minute into their latest contest.

"Only because you continue to lack subtlety and react too quickly to feints," Nest chided. "That and I have twenty centimeters and more kilos than I care to admit on you. Even so, what happened to that woman last week who took me down hard?"

Sparrow fought not to frown. It had been Lola who had taken Nest down last week, breaking through Sparrow's control just long enough to do it. It had been all she could do to stop the cold-blooded assassin inside her from killing Nest, and the experience had horrified her. She didn't often lose control of one of her...personalities, but when it happened, it was always disconcerting at best and terrifying at worst. She'd controlled it far better today, but the moment of hesitation it had caused her had lost her the bout.

She also frowned at the reference to her size. Sparrow had always been a little self-conscious about her diminutive stature. It put her at a disadvantage to her fellow agents in the Confederate Guard and was a constant source of ribbing from some of the less mature ones. That it actually often helped her in undercover assignments—no one suspected the short, skinny, shy-looking Latina of being a ruthless spy and assassin—was beside the point. Plus, Victoria often used it to great effect—she felt that tall and muscular women often intimidated men. But when it came to hand-to-hand combat of any kind, Sparrow—even with Lola in control—was at a severe disadvantage with anyone larger who had even close to the same amount of training as her.

Which Nest certainly had—more, actually. The Koratan Confederate Guard, the Confederacy's most elite direct action service that reported only to the star nation's sitting president, would have been well known for training highly proficient killers if most people didn't think it was all a myth. Nest had been an agent for almost two decades longer than Sparrow and was infinitely more well-trained, even without the size advantage. But Sparrow was slowly catching up, even when she didn't let Lola out to play.

"You'll want to get that cut looked at," Nest said. There was no sympathy in her tone, but Sparrow liked to think she said it because she was worried about her. "A scar will draw too much attention to your face." Nope, there it was. Typically, Nest wasn't worried about her underling, just the mission.

"I'll see to it right away, boss," she replied, pressing a towel to her cut cheek to stem the worst of the bleeding as she watched Nest stuff gauze up both nostrils to stop her nose from further gushing.

"Now that we're done with that, let's talk about your next assignment," Nest said almost casually, but there was an unusual edge to her voice that made Sparrow pause and pay even closer attention. In the back of her head, Katarina perked up, and even Trina turned her focus to the conversation while Lola listened from the shadows as she always did. Only Victoria ignored it all, still asleep in her usual place.

"How much do you know about la primera dama?" Nest asked.

That question took Sparrow aback. "The first lady?" She thought for a moment. Of course, she knew all about the wife of the Koratan president, and whatever she didn't know from memory was saved in her implant for quick and easy access. But by the tone of Nest's question, she didn't think the older woman was interested in the first lady's measurements, favorite foods, or taste in music, all of which were in the files the Guard kept on her.

No, she was digging for something more.

Sparrow shrugged. "I know she's not Koratan by birth and that she resents her husband."

The last part drew a sharp look from Nest. "Careful what you say," she admonished. "Even within these walls…especially within these walls. Her husband is our boss, and he is not a man known for appreciating those who speak negatively of him behind his back."

Sparrow shrugged again, not pressing the issue but not exactly apologizing either. Instead, she simply waited for her boss to get to the point, though Trina was quickly losing interest in the conversation.

Finally, Nest continued. "You do not share this with anyone else, understood?" She didn't wait for her underling to acknowledge; it was a question that required no answer. "We have intelligence that suggests the Prometheans are sending someone to kill the first lady before the election."

Sparrow couldn't help it; her composure broke, and she gasped. "Kill her? Why?" She left the rest of the question unsaid; they could both likely imagine exactly why the Prometheans, their long-standing enemies, would want the president himself dead. He had, just three weeks before, tried to turn the 300-year-old cold war between their nations into a very hot one. In reality, it would be surprising if the Prometheans *weren't* planning some sort of aggressive retaliation—even though the man was likely to be voted out of office anyway in the next month's election—if only to send a message. But going after the man's wife made no sense; she wasn't political, not really, preferring to stay on the family estate on Serenidad even when her husband was on Koratas engaged in the business of ruling the star nation.

Nest studied her and undoubtedly saw through her to the thoughts she kept unvoiced but said nothing to call her out on them. "The why is unimportant," she said a moment later. "It's the who that concerns us."

At the older woman's tone, even Trina snapped back to full attention so that Sparrow had to struggle momentarily with the other woman to keep her from taking control. Trina did that sometimes; she was flighty and easily distracted, but when she focused hard on something, she almost automatically asserted dominance in Sparrow's head.

"We have it on good authority," Nest said slowly, hopefully oblivious to her underling's inner battle, "that they're sending la Cruz del Rey."

Sparrow's breath caught, and she could feel Lola's excitement next to Katarina's surprise and even fear. Everyone in the Guard knew the reputation of the vaunted King's Cross, of course. They were supposed to be the Promethean equivalent of the Confederate Guard. There were even rumors they might be better, though no one Sparrow knew actually believed those.

Still, there had long been an unspoken agreement between the two warring star nations that their greatest strategic weapons, the Guard and the King's Cross—both groups of elite, purpose-trained assassins—were never to be used directly against each other's heads of state.

The first lady of the Koratan Confederacy wasn't exactly the head of state, but she was close enough that sending the King's Cross after her signaled a major shift in Promethean policy. It also made absolutely no sense.

She wanted to ask Nest again why the Prometheans wanted the president's wife dead, but she held her tongue and continued to listen.

"If the intel is true, and we believe it is," the older woman resumed speaking, "then only the Guard has a hope of stopping the assassination."

Sparrow nodded, but Katarina prodded her. "I agree, boss, but I do have one question. If the King's Cross is involved, that means it's being planned by the Promethean King himself, so how did we find out about it? We don't have anyone that close to the King, do we?"

Something flashed in Nest's eyes that was gone so quickly that Sparrow may have imagined it. "The source of our intelligence is not your concern," the senior agent said evenly. "But stopping the assassination from happening is your next mission."

"Me?" Sparrow asked, the statement surprising her so much that she almost lost control to Katarina or Trina—they were both fighting for dominance at that very moment, excited by what they were hearing.

"Not you alone," Nest clarified, which made more sense.

Sparrow was a relatively junior agent, even if she was racking up a kill count already that rivaled many of her more experienced peers. Of course, if they knew she was so effective because she literally had four other agents living in her head with her, then they'd probably lock her up and throw away the proverbial key. Still, no matter how effective she was, she was young and lacked seasoning, so it would have been shocking in the extreme for her to be solely placed in charge of saving the first lady's life.

"You'll be working for El Lobo," Nest said next, eyeing Sparrow closely.

Katarina and Trina abruptly shied back, their sudden retreat from their fight for control almost causing Sparrow's composure to crumble completely. As it was, Nest probably saw the widening of her eyes and quickening of her breath as a simple reaction to the news.

El Lobo—Wolf—was by a very large margin not Sparrow's favorite agent to be around, much less work with. That he would be placed in charge of protecting the first lady from the King's Cross made sense—he specialized in counterintelligence, the Guard's fancy way of saying he was good at killing enemy agents—but the man was...difficult. Of her personalities, only Lola came somewhere close to liking Wolf, and it was more professional respect than anything more. Even Lola had to admit that Wolf lacked even the basic scruples that most Guard agents had. Sure, they might be sent often to do the president's dirty work, but most of them drew some hard lines as to the type of missions they would take on. Koratas, after all, wasn't Prometheus, and the president wasn't a king.

But Wolf had never seemed to have any moral quandaries about anything he'd been asked to do. There were rumors even that he had killed several children in his career when they'd either been tagged as targets or simply gotten between him and his mission. Sparrow believed the rumors; the man seemed devoid of any conscience.

Katarina thought it was because he was a sociopath. Trina thought he was just a jerk. Lola agreed somewhat with Katarina but thought as well that Wolf simply liked the challenges that came with the dirty work. Victoria thought he was hot, but none of them listened to her anyway on matters of male character.

"I know you dislike him," Nest said, reading her protégé's expression. "But he specifically requested you, Raven, and Fox. He gave no explanation as to why, but you should consider it an honor to have been chosen for such a prestigious assignment. Of course, that only counts if you succeed." She left the rest unsaid; failure in a mission like this would likely result in more than Sparrow's firing from the Guard.

"You are to report to him in two hours for your briefing. This assignment is so secret that not even I will be privy to his plans, and you are to report to him and only him until the conclusion of the mission." The way Nest said the last part belied her own dark feelings toward the male agent.

I don't like this, Trina said, almost frantically. *This isn't good, chica. That hombre is always watching. What if he figures us out?*

Sparrow shoved Trina back down before the woman's fear could translate to her face. "I hear and obey. For the Guard," she said to cover it up, using the formal response to accept a mission.

Nest nodded but frowned, studying Sparrow so closely that she was momentarily terrified that she'd let something slip.

But then she relaxed marginally when the older woman reached out and put a hand on her shoulder. "You'll do fine, Sparrow. I know you'll make us all proud."

FOUR
A MARRIAGE OF CONVENIENCE

NANETTE FOURNIER DE IGNACIO

Nanette Fournier was not a happy woman. Indeed, she hadn't been entirely happy since the day, 20 long years ago, when her mother had announced her impending nuptials.

It hadn't been surprising that her mother had chosen her husband for her. Nanette had always known that would be the case. As the second oldest child of the Duchess of Nouveau Bourbon, a small, largely inconsequential single-system star nation, it had always been a foregone conclusion that she would be married not for love but for political advantage. It was her duty, just as her older brother, Francois, would eventually do his duty and take their mother's place as the system's ruler.

Nouveau Bourbon was a relatively unimportant system, with little to speak of in terms of exports, economy, or even trade with outside star nations. Except for one thing: its location. Situated in the Fringe but near the borders of two Outer Rim Star Nations—the Clancy Republic and the Euro-Prussian Union—Nanette's homeworld found itself almost by accident at a strategic crossroads and had played host to many summits and meetings over the years between Fringe nations and their Outer Rim cousins.

Therefore, Nanette, like her uncle before her, grew up always knowing that she would be married off to some aristocrat or up-and-coming politician in some neighboring star nation. She'd come to accept it early on, refusing to even date as a teenager despite many suitors, not willing to put herself in a position where she might fall in love only to have it end in disappointment.

Despite all that, when her mother finally did announce her marriage, she expected not to be upset about it. That was, of course, until she announced to *whom* Nanette would be wed.

Her first meeting with Francisco Ignacio Juarez had been a cold one. The man was in his mid-twenties at the time, the son of a soon-to-be-retiring Koratan senator and a fast-rising star in the Confederacy's political arena in his own right. He was tall, with a thin but well-built frame, and had lush black hair and a chiseled jaw that made him the darling of the Koratan media; a potential future presidential run was already being discussed even as he took his first seat in the star nation's congress. In press conferences and interviews, he was bold but self-deprecating, a true man of the people while still exuding a dignified and sometimes even aristocratic air when it suited him.

None of this was on display the first time he met his soon-to-be wife. When Nanette's mother introduced her to the Koratan politician, Francisco looked her up and down like he was examining a cut of meat at market and then sniffed and proclaimed her 'suitable'. Throughout the entire meeting, he never addressed her once directly, speaking exclusively to her mother, almost as if Nanette weren't even in the room.

The next three months of their engagement and the subsequent two decades of marriage since had changed the man in no perceptible way, except that as he'd climbed the ranks of political power—eventually becoming president of the Koratan Confederacy—he'd become even more aloof from his wife, making it abundantly clear that she was little more than arm candy and window dressing.

If Nanette's story reads like the plot of a bad romance novel, in which the heroine stays obstinately opposed to her cold and distant husband, eventually finding herself and true love in the process, then the reader is in for disappointment. Nanette, seeing no other options, subdued herself to Francisco's will, living a life of solitude even surrounded by her husband's staff and servants. On their public outings, usually to fundraisers, fancy dinner parties, or the occasional showy visit to a charity where she and Francisco would pretend to help out for the benefit of the cameras, she stayed largely silent, speaking only when following the script provided by her husband's handlers.

Nanette Fournier, now Fournier de Ignacio by marriage, was alone and almost entirely depressed for 11 full years under Francisco's thumb. Then, she got pregnant.

The pregnancy was a surprise, especially to her. Despite being married for over a decade, Francisco and Nanette had made love only a handful of times. She knew he kept mistresses and even hired call girls but had always done her best to ignore the other women, which was made easier by the fact that she bore no love for her husband and really didn't care if he never touched her. Still, things happen, and after one of the few times they did sleep together, she became pregnant with a baby girl.

Estrella Ignacio Fournier may have borne her father's last name first in true Koratan tradition but had otherwise inherited little from the man. While she had taken the best physical traits of both her parents, those who saw her often commented on how much she favored her mother. The one exception was that she had her father's lush black hair, which, coupled with her mother's light blue eyes, provided a contrast that made her the favorite of popular culture throughout the Confederacy. But, in Nanette's opinion—biased though it may have been by a mother's love—Estrella's physical beauty as a child did not compare in the least to the beauty of her soul.

Estrella—'star' in English—was a kind and gentle child from the start. She had a level of empathy surprising for one so young and sang with the voice of an angel when it could be coaxed out of her. A child of few words but with an emotive face and eyes, her shyness didn't stop her from having the entirety of her father's staff wrapped around her little finger without even trying. Her father, in fact, may have been the only living being in the galaxy immune to his daughter's silent charms.

With a husband who did not love her and a life that did not suit her, Nanette found her first joy and happiness in years in bringing up her daughter. She poured everything she had into raising Estrella, showing her first backbone in her marriage by utterly refusing to allow Francisco to hire a nanny or tutors. Instead, Nanette cared for and taught the little girl herself, cherishing even the moments when the child—as children often do—threatened to get on her nerves.

For a woman who had had a life devoid of love—even her own parents had often treated her more as a political pawn than a true daughter—Nanette was almost overwhelmed by the love she felt for Estrella, and especially by the love the little girl gave back to her in equal or greater measure.

"Mamá," Estrella said, wrapping her arms around Nanette's waist and hugging her tightly. "Do we have to go?"

Nanette frowned down at her nine-year-old daughter and nodded, trying not to look sad. "It will only be for a couple of months, my little star. Your father needs us back on Koratas."

The little girl frowned but didn't argue, instead looking

around at her room in the family's estate on Serenidad, where she and her mother lived most of the year while her father ruled the Confederacy from the presidential palace on Koratas itself. Now that Francisco Ignacio Juarez had achieved his star nation's highest office, he preferred his family not to be around while he governed, and Nanette and her daughter had been all too happy to oblige by staying on Serenidad usually for nine months out of the standard year.

But now, they'd been summoned back to the capital, not because Francisco particularly wanted them with him, but because his handlers and advisers felt that the image of him as a family man was needed after the fiasco at Hudson.

After all, Nanette's fool of a husband had sent the entirety of the Koratan Navy's Third Fleet to Hudson on the contested Harper Line. With an election looming and his poll numbers plummeting—he'd been embroiled in several high-profile scandals and had even been caught with one of his mistresses by the press corps—he'd been willing to do *anything* to resolidify his power, even if it meant starting a shooting war that would cost millions or even billions of lives.

Nanette suspected there was far more to it than that. Francisco was a vain and self-absorbed man, but even he could be trusted to make rational decisions and choose what would benefit him the most. The desperation that the failed attack at Hudson displayed was unlike that of her cold and calculating husband. Even *he* had to have known that, while it may have gotten him reelected as a wartime president, the rise in popularity would be short-lived after the first deaths were reported.

Despite all that, Francisco had still used his little remaining influence among the Koratan bicameral congress—no doubt blackmailing many of them with the dirt he used the Confederate Guard to gather—and had garnered just enough votes to send the fleet to Hudson. Of course, the official and authorized reason had been for a 'show of power', to demonstrate to the Prometheans that the contested territory belonged more to Koratas than it did to them. But, unbeknownst even to most of his closest allies in Congress, Ignacio Juarez had other plans. Conspiring with Third Fleet's commander, Admiral Juanita Torres—a woman who shared her president's rabid lust for power—Francisco sent the fleet there not to show strength but to start a fight.

The plan had been simple: send the fleet, let them skirt the treaty line and 'accidentally' cross into the inner system at Hudson, and then use the Promethean Navy's inevitable response as an excuse to start a war. Torres assured her president that the Promethean system commander at Hudson, Rear Admiral Christoph Turly, would not only take the bait but would probably escalate things by calling in the Promethean Second Fleet, though it would be too late to prevent Hudson and likely the rest of the Harper Line from falling into uncontested Koratan hands.

The plan seemed simple despite its insanity, but somehow, it leaked, and the Promethean Navy's Second Fleet was already waiting at Hudson when Admiral Torres and Third Fleet arrived. The invasion failed before it could start, and the subsequent leak of President Ignacio Juarez's full plans had even his allies in Congress calling for a vote of no confidence. The only thing that prevented such a vote was the upcoming election—less than four weeks away now—in which Francisco was expected to lose by a landslide.

In response, his political advisors—the ones who hadn't already abandoned him—were calling for a full-court press in the media, part of which was parading the man's wife and daughter in front of the cameras to garner sympathy for the embattled president.

Nanette had little choice but to go to Koratas and be Francisco's window dressing, but she vowed to herself that she would keep her daughter out of the spotlight as much as possible. Now, she took the little girl's hand and followed her own chief of staff—employed by and obedient to her husband, not her—toward the entrance to the estate grounds and the small shuttle that would take them into orbit to the waiting Koratan Navy destroyer that would transport mother and daughter to Koratas and away from any happiness they may have otherwise had.

FIVE
PICKING UP A TAIL
HEATHER KILGORE

Heather stopped in front of a small mirror that let tourists try on sunglasses on the busy street of La Ciudad Delgado on Santa Maria IV. Delgado wasn't the planet's capital city, but it was one of its major business and commerce centers and drew crowds from across the planet and from nearby systems for its shopping and entertainment. And if one thing was a constant in any Koratan tourist center, it was the abundance of street vendors.

Heather grabbed a pair of sunglasses from the rack and tried them on, studying the image in the mirror. Besides quickly noting that the glasses were too wide for her face, she also saw the man who had been following her for the last two blocks as he quickly turned aside and tried to appear like he was browsing the wares of another street vendor 20 meters behind her.

Idiot. Either the man in his slick business suit and expensive tie was really a fan of healing crystals, or he had simply picked the booth closest to him to try and escape her notice. For a supposed professional—though she still wasn't 100%

sure who he worked for—he was rather bad at this counterintelligence stuff.

Of course, he couldn't be *all* bad. He had found *her*, even if he was doing a terrible job tailing her. And that was worrisome. Santa Maria IV was still four jumps away from Serenidad, Heather's eventual destination. That she had picked up a tail at all this far from her objective didn't bode well for her mission, and she tried hard to think of what slip-up she may have committed that somehow allowed the Koratans to identify her.

Or maybe…

Kilgore put the sunglasses back on the rack and started moving again, pretending she hadn't noticed the man behind her. She made straight for a line of food trucks across the wide boulevard. Traffic was heavy at this hour, so she threaded her way through the mostly stopped vehicles, drawing a few angry glares from drivers even though they couldn't have moved their cars in the dense gridlock even without her presence. But she gave them a new target for their wrath; one even honked at her.

She heard another honk as she reached the opposite sidewalk, no doubt a motorist upset with her pursuer as he stepped into the street to follow her. Heather didn't look back but ducked between two of the food trucks, one serving tacos and the other something called frybread. Each had long lines, and she cut through one of them and then leapt up a short set of steps to an apartment doorway, her implant quickly hacking the cheap lock so that it admitted her into the vestibule. She closed the door behind her and stood to one side, peering through the dirty glass.

Sure enough, ten seconds later, the man following her came into view, standing on his toes and peering up and down the row of food trucks as if he were trying to find her in one of the lines. She could see him frowning, but he never once looked at the window through which she was watching him. Her estimation of his skills dropped even lower.

Heather watched as he started making his way through the crowd away from her before she opened the outer door again and ducked out, now following behind him. He looked back a couple of times as if to ensure he hadn't missed her in one of the food truck lines, but each time she was able to keep a hungry patron between them and his eyes never fixed on her.

When he rounded the corner, she stopped and waited in case he decided to double back. After a minute, he hadn't, and she peered around the corner, pleased to see that he was still walking 30 meters down the next block, searching for her.

She followed him like that for another two blocks, including a turn or two as he desperately sought his quarry, before it became clear that the man was giving up. He stopped looking around and started walking faster and on a more direct route, no doubt headed back to his home base or safe house to report his failure to his masters. She hoped it wouldn't be a fun conversation for the man.

Six blocks later, he turned into another apartment building. Heather waited for the door to close behind him but didn't follow. Instead, she ducked into the shadow of a doorway on the opposite side of the street and watched the building closely.

It was a brownstone, common enough on any Fringe world, though it was constructed from a local rock that was more black than anything else. She idly wondered why it was always called a 'brownstone' no matter what the actual color was but shoved the thought aside and kept up her vigil.

Five minutes later, she was rewarded with the sight of movement on the third floor as the man who had been following her stepped to the window and peered out casually at the street below. At first, she thought he might be doing so to scan for any followers like her, but her implant optics allowed her to zoom in and see that his eyes didn't even move to sweep the street. A couple of seconds later, he turned and retreated from the window.

Heather smiled to herself. Was it really going to be this easy?

She stayed there for two more hours, though she made sure to move to different parts of the street every so often in case the man was more watchful than she suspected, but always where she had a view of the brownstone's front door. She even changed her appearance a few times, using a skullcap to hide her hair, which was dyed black—her natural auburn hair would have been horribly out of place on predominantly Latino Koratan worlds like this one, even if many of the young women seemed to enjoy dyeing their hair an artificial red.

Finally, her patience was rewarded when the man left through the front door and made his way down the block and around a corner. She waited a few minutes to ensure he was gone and then made her move.

His door control was more sophisticated than most—in fact, it was on par with some of the best commercial models she'd seen—but it couldn't stand up to her implant's hacking capabilities and delayed her for no more than a few moments. But when she reached out and grasped the door handle to turn it, she stopped. It wouldn't budge in her hand, and no amount of twisting or pushing on the door could get it to open despite the green light on the electronic lock that signaled it was disengaged.

She studied the door more closely and noticed for the first time a slightly discolored patch. Flicking out her knife, she used the tip to pry at the patch and quickly found its edge to see it easily swung aside like a small door, revealing an old-fashioned keyhole underneath.

How quaint. But in a world of electronic security, it was also very effective. The typical thief or even lesser spy would have to turn away at this point or risk breaking down the door and drawing attention to themselves. However, Heather was neither thief nor lesser spy, and she sheathed her knife and then reached down to remove a multi-tool from her pocket. A moment later, she had successfully picked the lock and the door swung open.

Once inside, she surveyed the modest-sized space. It was devoid of personal effects. There were no pictures and no books or bits of paper that might have revealed the man's identity. Which, in and of itself, was unusual enough to tell her much about him. This was definitely not the place he lived, more likely a temporary safe house, and by the light layer of dust covering most of the flat surfaces and the mostly empty trash cans, he hadn't been here more than a day or two at most.

The bed was neatly made, and Heather was tired—the day's events before the man had tried to follow her had drained her more than anticipated, and the skin of her stomach hurt fiercely. She opened her duffel and pulled out her simplest yet most effective security tool—even more effective than the physical lock the apartment's owner had relied on so much—a small wedge of wood. She stuck it under the apartment's front door to prevent it from opening, then laid down on top of the bed and was quickly asleep, her duffel and its other precious contents under one arm.

SIX
THE BIRD AND THE WOLF
SPARROW

Sparrow still couldn't explain fully why she disliked Wolf so much.

It's because he's an asesino, Trina said sullenly inside her head.

We're all killers, replied Katarina, ever the practical one. *Well, at least Lola is. But we help.*

Yeah, but that garoto enjoys it too much, Victoria said. Even she couldn't relax enough to get much sleep in the other agent's presence. *Even if he is muito bonito,* she added unnecessarily.

Lola, characteristically, only grunted, though it wasn't clear what part of the conversation she was agreeing with.

"No harm can come to the first lady," Wolf was saying now, moving his cold gaze between Sparrow and the two other agents assembled in the small briefing room.

Raven, to Sparrow's left, was a man in his thirties, probably the same age as Wolf, but who specialized in the protection of high-value assets. Fox, to her right, was a woman just a few years older than Sparrow, who specialized in urban combat tactics. While the Guard was mostly a small group of very independent operators, occasionally, they did have to take command of police units, SWAT teams, or even military units, and Fox usually headed up those efforts.

To Sparrow, it made perfect sense why both Fox and Raven were here. They would each thrive on a mission that required detecting a threat and using local resources to counter it. But what she couldn't figure out was why she was here. Sparrow specialized in finding and taking out targets—she was an assassin, plain and simple—but she had no experience detecting threats or working with others to protect anyone.

Maybe he thinks we're cute, Victoria said, her voice a mixture of excitement and disgust that Sparrow really didn't want to unpack right now.

"In two days, Nanette Fournier de Ignacio will be on Koratas and will remain here until election day," Wolf continued. "While she is here, she will be staying at the presidential palace."

Raven raised a hand. "Will her normal security team be watching her there?"

Wolf's lip curled up in a subtle sneer. "Yes, but I believe they are already too complacent, and we are dealing with an agent of the King's Cross. Even the palace itself is not a perfectly safe place. So one of you," he pointed first to Raven and then to Fox, "will remain with her at all times, taking alternating shifts, even while she is safe at home. Then you will both accompany her to any public appearances, supplementing and directing the efforts of her security team." He looked hard at Fox. "Make them understand that the Guard is in charge of Señora Fournier's safety, and they are to follow any command we give them without question. Clear?"

Fox nodded but said nothing. She tended to be quiet; Sparrow had never heard the taciturn woman say any more than was necessary, sort of like Lola.

"Good," Wolf continued. Between now and when she arrives, I want all of us to work out scenarios of how the King's Cross agent might try to kill the first lady. We will review them tomorrow afternoon and choose those we believe are most likely so we can build contingency plans to counter them."

Despite not liking the man in front of them, Sparrow felt Katarina getting excited at the prospect of making plans and counter plans.

"Dismissed!" Wolf finished.

Raven and Fox got up obediently to leave, but Sparrow lingered despite wanting to escape the room and Wolf's presence as quickly as possible. When the other two agents were gone, Wolf looked at her, a challenge in his eyes, but said nothing.

"Uh, may I ask you a question, sir?"

He gave her a curt nod but remained silent.

"You gave assignments to Fox and Raven but not to me. What will I be doing?"

For the first time that day, Wolf smiled. It wasn't a nice smile—far too many teeth—nor did it reach his eyes. "Simple, Agent Sparrow, you will be with me." He looked at her as if that were explanation enough.

"Doing what, sir?" she pressed.

"What you do best, of course," he said, his smile getting broad but no more friendly. "Hunting. You and I, Agent Sparrow, we are going to hunt this agent of the King's Cross and kill them before they even get to Koratas."

SEVEN
THE ANALYST

HEATHER KILGORE

When Heather awoke to the sound of a man swearing, it was already dark outside. She could hear her mysterious pursuer struggling at his own apartment door, issuing invectives against it for its refusal to open. She got up and moved to it, where she let him wind down and stop pushing on it. Then, she used her foot to move the small wooden doorstop out of the way. When he tried again, he pushed so hard that he practically fell inside when it opened with no resistance, ending up on his hands and knees, staring up at the borehole of Heather's pistol.

"It's you!" he cried in astonishment.

In reply, she held up a finger in front of her lips. The man nodded his understanding and got slowly to his feet, keeping his hands up where she could see them and then using his foot to close the door behind him.

"Take your gun out slowly," she told him in a low voice once the door was shut. "Two fingers, keep away from the trigger. Toss it onto the couch."

"But I'm…" he trailed off and thought better of whatever

argument he'd planned when she speared him with a look. So, he did as instructed.

"Good, now the one in the ankle holster as well."

His eyes flashed surprise and annoyance, but he complied.

"You know, the ankle holster makes you walk funny. It's obvious to anyone watching that you have a hideaway weapon," she told him. "Like the knife in your sleeve, which, by the way, is holstered pointing in the wrong direction to do any good. Take that out too, slowly."

He frowned at her but again followed her orders.

"Good," she said. "Now, tell me why ProSec is interfering with my mission."

Now, the man looked truly surprised, but he didn't get angry. He let go of a long sigh and shrugged, his hands still held high where she could see them. "They told me not to underestimate you. I guess I should have listened."

Heather didn't reply. Given the guy's clumsy tradecraft, she was certain he couldn't have done much better even if he *had* tried his hardest, but she chose not to tell him that.

"Tell me why ProSec is interfering with my mission," she said again, her voice harder. ProSec was the Promethean Security Service, the second-most effective intelligence agency in their star nation behind the Order—a very distant second.

He frowned again. "I'm going to ping something to your implant, OK?"

She didn't reply but accepted the ping and opened the file once her implant notified her it was free of any threats.

"It's an addendum to your orders," he told her unnecessarily. "Straight from the top."

"I usually don't take orders from ProSec," she replied. It was true; the Order of the King's Cross took orders from *no one* apart from the King himself. She'd never heard of ProSec even being used to pass those orders along.

He shrugged again. "Check the authentication codes. I think you'll find everything is legit."

Heather had already done so, and they *were* legitimate, at least on the surface. She would do a deeper check later. For now, she was still trying to determine what the update to orders meant.

"The president's wife and daughter won't be on Serenidad when you get there," he said, for some reason feeling the need to tell her what the orders he'd sent her already had. "They're headed to…Koratas."

She frowned at him. Had he just paused for dramatic effect? It was a wonder ProSec got anything done with idiots like this working for them.

"I can see that. But why not wait until they're back at Serenidad? Koratas is the capital planet; it's the last place we want to try and assassinate members of the presidential family." That was one thing that *wasn't* in the new orders: the reason for the change.

He shrugged, starting to lower his hands, but raised them again at a sharp glance from her. "They didn't tell me, but if I had to speculate, I'd say it's because President Ignacio Juarez is under a lot of fire right now for the failed invasion at Hudson. He's probably bringing his family to the capital to help his image. His wife's approval rating is a lot higher than his, and the daughter's is *way* up there. So he's likely to keep them on the planet until after the election, and we need to kill them before the vote."

Heather shook her head. Approval ratings? It was something she largely never needed to care about in a monarchy, where even Parliament was primarily made up of nobles who got their jobs based on their parents, not some popular vote.

Plus, this guy wasn't telling her anything she couldn't have figured out on her own. Even the part about the first lady and her daughter going to Koratas would have eventually been on the news. So why was he really here?

"Can I put my hands down?" he asked her sheepishly, interrupting her thoughts.

"You can, but make a single move I don't like, and I'll kill you. No warnings." Despite her words, she lowered the gun slightly so that it was only vaguely pointed in his direction.

He chuckled as he lowered his hands but then gulped as he caught her dark look. "OK. I, uh, guess you're not joking. Do they force King's Cross agents to surrender their sense of humor?"

She ignored his lame attempt at lightening the mood.

"My name is Brighton, Zak," he said next, reaching out a hand in greeting.

Heather looked at it sourly but didn't take it. He looked at her expectantly. She looked back into his eyes and made no move to respond to his implied question.

"And your name is?" he asked, not taking the hint.

"They didn't give you my name in your briefing packet?" she asked.

"No, they didn't," he admitted.

"So then, tell me why my new orders say you're supposed to work with me on this?"

He looked sheepish. "They thought I might be able to help you."

"How? Your tradecraft is terrible. How long have you been an agent?"

If anything, he looked even more sheepish, and his face started to flush. "Um, I'm actually *not* an agent. I'm an analyst."

Heather felt her eyes go wide in surprise. "They sent an *analyst* to help me with a job behind enemy lines? Whose stupid idea was that?"

Now he was *really* red, and he just shrugged.

Without another word, she stepped around him—her precious duffle was already over one shoulder—and started heading toward the door, walking backward now so that she could keep her eyes on him, her gun still pointed in his general direction.

"You're leaving? Just like that?" he asked, his eyebrows knit in confusion as he turned to face her again. "But I'm supposed to go with you."

Heather said nothing but kept walking back toward the closed door, reaching behind herself to open it and turning her body so she could peer outside while keeping the ProSec agent in her peripheral vision.

The man—Zak Brighton—took a step forward but stopped as her gun twitched upward. "I mean, it's orders. I'm supposed to stay with you and help you," he tried arguing again.

Heather stopped right before going out the apartment door, eying him skeptically. "If I ever see you again," she said somberly, "you'll be dead before you ever see me."

The blood drained from his face, and he visibly gulped. It was the last she saw of him before she closed the door behind her.

EIGHT
LITTLE STAR
ESTRELLA IGNACIO FOURNIER

Estrella was only nine, but that meant most people thought she was a lot dumber than she really was. The fact that she didn't talk much made them think she wasn't listening either. But Estrella was *always* listening...and watching.

Like now, she watched her mamá fidget in the seat next to her as they waited outside her father's office. They'd been there for a really long time. When they'd started, the small hand on the room's wall clock had been on the one. Now, it was past the two. Estrella was getting tired and hungry; they'd been on the ship for three days, and it had just arrived before they came to her father's office. They didn't even have time to stop at their rooms or get a snack.

But worse, Estrella could tell that Mamá wasn't happy. Mamá was never happy around Father. And Father was never happy, period. Sure, she'd seen him smile, but that didn't mean he was happy. People smiled all the time around Estrella without actually being happy about anything. Like her father's secretary, a man who reminded her of a weasel she'd seen once in her garden on Serenidad. He kept smiling at Mamá and telling her it would only be a few more minutes, but he definitely wasn't happy. Because whenever Mamá wasn't looking, he frowned and tried really hard to look busy.

Estrella wasn't happy either right now. Not only was she tired and hungry, but she couldn't be happy when Mamá wasn't happy. Regardless, she said nothing and didn't complain. It would just make Mamá sadder if Estrella complained.

The office's inner door finally opened, and a group of men and women filed out. None of them looked happy, either, most frowning openly and refusing to even look at Estrella and her mamá. All except for kind old Señor Jonas, whom Estrella had known for her entire life. He stopped when he saw her and Mamá sitting there and came over to them, crouching down in front of Estrella.

"My little star," he said, smiling at her. "It is good to see you. I have something for you." He reached into the pocket of his suit coat, pulled out a chocolate candy, and handed it to her. Estrella smiled and took it, even though it wasn't enough to make her happy. But she didn't want Señor Jonas or Mamá to look any sadder, so she pretended to be satisfied with the little gift.

"How is he today?" Mamá asked Sr. Jonas in a low voice, peering toward the office door, which was still open a little bit.

Sr. Jonas frowned. "It's been a bad day, Señora. The Speaker of the House commed earlier to say that his own party will withdraw their support for his reelection. He is still…digesting it."

Mamá frowned back at Sr. Jonas. "Is there anything he can do?"

The older man smiled sadly. "Go back in time and not send the fleet to Hudson, perhaps?" Then he shook his head. "No, I'm afraid the die is cast."

Estrella had no idea what that meant. What did a cast have to do with anything? Did Father break a bone?

"All we can do now is try and salvage some of his reputation," continued Sr. Jonas. "Perhaps you and the little star here can help with that."

Estrella saw Mamá look suddenly angry, but then she looked down at her daughter and saw Estrella looking up at her, and her face became calmer. She opened her mouth to say something else to Sr. Jonas, but a loud voice interrupted from inside the office door.

"Nanette, get in here!" the voice of Estrella's father yelled. He sounded angry, which was normal for him. Father almost always sounded angry when he talked to Mamá or Estrella. He only sounded happy when he talked on the news or in front of big groups of people.

Estrella's mamá sighed and stood up, straightening her dress and giving a small smile to Estrella that looked very fake. "Watch her for me?" she said to Sr. Jonas, who frowned and nodded.

"Nanette!" Father's voice yelled again.

Mamá turned and marched toward the office, entering and shutting the door behind her. Sr. Jonas watched her go and then turned to Estrella.

"Tell me, little star," he said kindly. "Have you learned your subtraction yet?"

She nodded, biting her lip to keep from crying. She wasn't even sure why she wanted to cry, but she did.

"Good. Can you tell me what seven minus four is?"

Estrella thought for a second and then answered. "That's easy, Tio Jonas. It's three."

He smiled at her. "Wonderful. How about a more difficult one? Twenty-four minus five."

She thought harder this time and was about to answer when she heard a muffled scream from the direction of the closed office door. She turned to stare at it, biting her lip again, harder this time. Sr. Jonas reached out and took both her hands.

"Estrella, look at me, OK? Twenty-four minus five."

She looked back at him. "It's…uh…it's 19?"

"Marvelous. Now, let's go for a walk out in the hall and do a few more, shall we?"

Estrella cast one more look at the closed office door, then at her father's secretary, who was sitting really low in his seat like he didn't want Estrella to see him behind his desk. She looked back at Sr. Jonas and nodded, still biting her lip.

He reached out and took her hand, helped her off the chair, and led her toward the outer door back into the big hallway. As he went, he gave her another math problem: "Forty-six minus 2."

As they left the waiting room, Estrella heard another scream behind them, but Sr. Jonas tugged on her hand and quickly pulled her out through the door, closing it behind him and cutting off any further sound from her father's office. "Forty-six minus 2," he reminded her.

"Forty-two."

"Try again, little star."

"Forty-four?"

"Ah, yes. So smart. Let's see if I can give you a harder one."

Estrella was still worried about Mamá, but the old man's calming voice and the hard math problems he gave her distracted her a little bit, and she let herself be led further and further from her father's office. Soon, she was waving a shy hello to other men and women in the building, who probably all worked for her father, as Sr. Jonas introduced her to them. A few she recognized, she thought, from her last time visiting the palace, but others she was pretty sure were new.

Her mamá found her with Sr. Jonas a long time later,

sitting and drinking hot cocoa in his office. Estrella gasped when she saw Mamá. There was a dark spot on her cheek and blood on the front of her dress.

Estrella started to cry as Mamá rushed to her and held her tight. Sr. Jonas just sat there, looking very sad as he watched mother and daughter embrace.

NINE
THE BEST DEFENSE
SPARROW

"Why Novo Recife?"

Sparrow looked up at Wolf's deep voice as they sat in the shuttle on its way to one of the many orbital stations above Koratas.

"Pardon me, señor?" she asked meekly, upset at herself that he made her so nervous.

"In one of the assassination plans you presented today, you said that if you were a Promethean assassin coming to kill the first lady, you would stop at Novo Recife first. Why?"

Sparrow knit her brows together in confusion. She'd explained all this already when they'd met with Raven and Fox and gone over their various scenarios for how they would go about executing the King's Cross agent's mission. But she decided not to point this out to Wolf.

Don't tell him it was my idea, Victoria urged unnecessarily. If Sparrow didn't want Nest, whom she trusted, to know about the voices in her head, she sure didn't want Wolf to know. He'd probably kill her slowly just to see if he could extract her various personalities and find the weak spots for each and every one of them. The thought made her involuntarily shudder.

She tried to cover it up by answering his question. "Sir, I would go through Novo Recife because if I was going to kill Señora Fournier de Ignacio, I would need her schedule first. And Novo Recife is the best place for me to possibly get it."

"But why? And how?"

She couldn't tell if he legitimately didn't remember what she'd said earlier, was testing her, or just wanted to talk it through. Either way, she answered. "Because outside of the government, the only organizations with access to the first lady's public appearance schedule are the news bureaus. And most of them have regional offices on Novo Recife, where they would keep copies of that schedule on their servers."

He didn't nod or shake his head but regarded her with the same cold stare he seemed to wear as a permanent expression. "The news bureaus have regional offices throughout the Confederacy, including on Koratas, do they not? And Novo Recife isn't the closest or even on a direct line from Promethean space to Koratas. It will be at least two jumps out of the assassin's way. So, I ask again: why there specifically?"

She gulped and fought the urge to shiver under his scrutiny. "Because they don't speak Spanish on Novo Recife… most of them don't, at least."

"Explain," he demanded again, though he didn't raise his voice.

"Well, sir, if I were infiltrating Confederacy space to kill the first lady, I would want to make sure I'm not being followed. Unless the assassin they chose is Latino, and we don't know if he or she is or not, they will stand out on most of our worlds as a foreigner. But on Novo Recife, where the culture and language are different from most Koratan worlds, any of our agents pursuing her are almost just as likely to stand out. Going there not only gets them to the news bureaus but also gives them an opportunity to detect and shake anyone on our side who has identified and is following them."

"You really believe the differences between the Latino cultures and mannerisms will be enough for this King's Cross agent to detect?" he argued, though his tone remained perfectly flat and neutral.

I tried to tell you it was a weak plan, Katarina whined. *He obviously hates it.*

You're just mad because Victoria came up with it and not you, Trina said back sharply—a little too sharply—belying her own anxiety and losing her normally snarky and even playful tone when ribbing Katarina.

Sparrow frowned, doing her best to ignore the two women as they continued to bicker. "I admit, sir, it's not the strongest argument. But you asked how I would do it—how I would kill the first lady. And I would look for every edge I could get, no matter how slight."

He studied her for a few very awkward moments that made even *Lola* nervous. She was under no illusions who would win if it ever came down to a fight between her and Wolf, and the icy gaze he now fixed on Sparrow gave nothing away as to whether he wanted to support her plan or kill her for wasting his time…

"I agree," he said simply, surprising her. "So, we are going to Novo Recife." Then he turned away from her and stared straight ahead, his eyes going out of focus as he interfaced with his implant, the conversation clearly over.

Sparrow should have felt good that the senior Guard agent agreed with her idea, but she only felt a deep pit in her stomach as she considered traveling for days in each direction with no company other than Wolf. Not only was he not a person she could choose to spend any more time with than absolutely necessary, but one of the reasons she liked working alone was so that no one would ever get close enough to observe her closely and possibly surmise that she wasn't alone in her own mind. If Wolf ever figured things out...

She thrust the unhelpful thought aside. She'd simply need to be on her guard until this was all over, and not just against unknown Promethean assassins. Sparrow would have to be sure that Wolf suspected nothing.

But in the back of her head, she could practically feel Lola considering, even craving, what would happen if she failed.

TEN
THE SENSE OF IT ALL
HEATHER KILGORE

The passenger liner had just 300 people aboard and could have fit another hundred. Apparently, Heather's destination wasn't one of the more popular planets in the Koratan Confederacy.

She wasn't flying first class with the private quarters that doing so would have afforded her. Her expense account for this mission was essentially bottomless, but spending that much money on a liner ticket would have made her stand out more than she would have liked. She also knew that the difference between success and failure in a mission like this often came down to how well one had slept the week before, so she also didn't fly coach.

Instead, Heather flew business class, her smart pantsuit making her blend in with the other faceless, harried business travelers around her, some of them clearly foreigners like her. And at least her wide seat lay flat and had a privacy shield that descended over it when she so desired, which she usually did.

The Journey from Santa Maria IV to Novo Recife was three days long, covering just two jumps, but with one system the liner had to circumnavigate almost entirely to get from one jump point to the next. A fast Navy transport or a warship could have done the entire thing in just under two days, but Heather didn't have the luxury of Navy travel this deep in enemy territory. Here, she had to do her best to blend in with everyone else, watching her fellow travelers closely all the while for any sign that they might be more than they appeared, like her.

Unfortunately, that was about all she could do during the three-day journey. Her new orders troubled her, and she had decided that it would be foolhardy to travel directly to Koratas before gathering more intel about the situation and the presidential family's sudden change in location. Her current target, Novo Recife, was a planet about halfway between Santa Maria IV and the Koratan capital, though not on a direct line. There was a regional command base there for the Koratan Navy, which would surely have all the intel she needed on the first family's activities. However, there was also a regional office for Galactic News Network, and while GNN wasn't likely to have *everything* the government had, it would have enough for her purposes. It would also be a much easier nut to crack.

The extra three days in transit gave Heather a lot of time to think, and it did little to lighten her mood about this particular mission. When the head of the Order of the King's Cross had come to Hudson to personally give her the King's kill order for Nanette Fournier de Ignacio and Estrella Ignacio Fournier—Heather had never been able to quite follow how Spanish last names traditionally worked, and it was weird that they were slightly different between mother and daughter—the orders to kill them had come as a shock. Not just because it was such a brash and risky mission but mostly because the reasons for it just made *no* sense to her.

She could understand King Charles wanting to kill President Francisco Ignacio Juarez; the man had tried to invade the Harper Line and challenge Promethean sovereignty. But she couldn't wrap her head around why the King would want the man's wife and daughter dead instead. Sure, it would send a message, but it would also undoubtedly start a full-fledged war if it was even *suspected* that Prometheus was involved in the killings. Not to mention that doing it right before an election could sway the Koratan vote in unanticipated ways that might not be advantageous for Prometheus.

Despite 300 years of conflict between the two star nations, there had been only a few thousand casualties on both sides for that entire period. Open war between the two Fringe superpowers would result in millions, possibly even billions, of deaths, and not just from the fighting. One of the first things both nations would try and do would be to cut each other's supply lines to and from their outer systems. While some human planets were self-sufficient and could survive just fine without interstellar trade, they were the exception, not the rule. The simple reality was that some planets terraformed very well while others didn't. Hundreds of millions or more would likely die on both sides from starvation or lack of access to medical supplies. Infrastructures would crumble in ways that would be felt for decades after.

It wasn't just all speculation, either. Fifty years before, two outer rim star nations—the Republic of Bialystok and the Melnyk Federation—had gone to war over mining rights to a border system. What started as a small skirmish in that system quickly expanded to a star-spanning conflict that resulted in almost five percent of their combined populations dying during the ten-year conflict. After that, another ten percent died over the next 20 years from the infrastructure damage, especially after a plague swept through several systems and the governments couldn't get medical supplies manufactured and to them in time.

And *those* two star nations had been relatively small—less than a dozen systems each—whereas Prometheus and Koratas combined to include *hundreds* of star systems. The casualties from a war between the two Fringe superpowers would be *much* higher.

King Charles *had* to know all of this. So why was he risking it just to 'send a message' to the Koratans about how upset their failed invasion had made him? It simply wasn't rational and felt drastically out of character for the usually more cautious monarch. Of course, he was the same King who had once ordered her to kill a ten-year-old boy to ensure he didn't follow in his father's treasonous footsteps, but even then, she'd at least understood the logic behind the order. Whereas now…no matter how many angles she examined her current mission from, she just couldn't fathom what the King was thinking.

Worse, on the rare occasions over the journey's three days when she was completely honest with herself, Heather had to admit that it almost didn't matter the reasons behind King Charles' orders. She didn't *want* to do this particular mission. The last time he'd ordered her to kill a child, and she'd done it, it had ended a years-long friendship with Tabitha Lowry. And while Heather had killed the older woman for the treason she'd committed stemming from that event, she'd also *sympathized* with her over that one particular instance.

Despite all that, she knew her doubts were futile. She was an agent of the King's Cross, the one organization that the Promethean monarch and his people trusted to be 100% loyal to the Crown. If they stopped doing so, it would be catastrophic…or so she'd always believed. But a little voice inside wouldn't let the matter drop. And Heather had to admit, that when the time came with Estrella Ignacio Fournier in her sights, she might not be able to pull the trigger.

That scared her more than anything else. Because if she wasn't a loyal King's Cross agent, then what was she?

She almost laughed darkly to herself in her business-class seat. Whoever had heard of a King's Cross agent with a conscience? Heather had been recruited from prison, where she was serving a sentence for the brutal murder of her step-father and had already killed other prisoners without remorse. That now, years later, she would develop feelings of guilt was surprising and concerning. No matter how innocent Fournier and her daughter were, they were still enemies of Prometheus. And her orders were clear: she must kill them both. To do otherwise would be to betray her sovereign, ignore the fact that the Order had saved her from a life in prison, and end the only life she'd ever felt like she belonged in.

She had to complete her mission, no matter how little she wanted to. But it would sure be helpful if she could at least begin to understand the King's reasoning behind it.

Her circling thoughts were interrupted one day out from Novo Recife as her almost automatic scan of the passengers around her first caught a familiar face.

Unlike Heather, ProSec Agent—no, *analyst*—Zak Brighton did *not* understand what it meant to be inconspicuous. He was traveling in first class, in the compartment just ahead of Heather's, where he got his own private room with a larger bed that converted into a couch when necessary.

She saw him before he saw her, though it was painfully obvious he was back in business class looking for her. Heather once again marveled at the man's poor tradecraft. When she was done marveling, she got pissed. It was hard enough being this far into Koratan territory, on her way to assassinate the Confederacy's first family; it was even harder with a ProSec idiot who didn't even belong in the field threatening to blow her cover just by being himself.

She knew she couldn't hide from him forever, though, so she decided to cut her losses and stop him from searching every compartment and seat for her. In fact, she was readying herself to get out of her seat and go intercept him when she caught sight of someone else taking a marked interest in the ProSec analyst.

Zak Brighton had been made, and by the look of the male Koratan agent with the hatchet face who got up from four rows behind Heather to follow him forward, the Promethean man would soon learn what the Kories did to foreign spies in their territory.

Heather had two options now. She could intervene and stop Brighton's impending death—she didn't even consider capture; he knew too much about her mission for her to let him be taken prisoner—or she could wait and see if the Koratan agent did what she'd already threatened Brighton she would do if she ever saw him again. With him dead, it would free her up to do what she did best: work alone. It would also tie up what was quickly becoming a very annoying loose end.

Protocol suggested a third road, that she somehow kill Brighton before the Koratan agent could. Either way, she had a decision to make.

Swearing loudly enough under her breath to draw a startled glance from the woman sitting next to her, Heather got up from her seat and made her way forward to where Brighton and the Koratan agent had disappeared through the hatch into first class. She first made sure her precious duffel was secure in its lock box above her seat.

ELEVEN
FINAL APPROACH

HEATHER KILGORE

"Damas y caballeros, we have just exited the jump point into Novo Recife and are making our way to the planet. We will dock with the Várzea orbital in nine hours. Please begin now to prepare for arrival."

Heather had tailed the hatchet-faced Koratan agent into first class over six hours ago and had watched as he walked right past the hatch to Brighton's cabin, giving it what appeared on the surface to be only a passing glance. Then he'd returned to his seat and stayed there ever since.

Now, however, as the captain's announcement replayed in Spanish and Portuguese, Heather saw the Koratan get up from his seat again and make a beeline for the first-class cabin. No doubt his plan was to confirm his suspicion of Brighton's status as a spy and then call ahead to the planet to ask for any needed support.

She waited a few moments until the hatch closed behind Hatchetface and then got up and followed. She didn't want him getting too far ahead of her. Brighton's first-class cabin supposedly had an implant-triggered lock on it and would only open for him or his designated guests, but the lock models on commercial starliners were almost laughingly easy to hack, and it wouldn't take the Koratan long to get inside and either question or kill the ProSec analyst.

Entering through the hatch into the first-class compartment, she followed the narrow corridor that went past the doors to the various cabins. The carpeted passageway doglegged ahead of her, and her quarry had already disappeared around the corner. As she poked her head around to find him, she saw him standing outside of a familiar cabin hatch, staring at it, clearly using his implant to hack it just as she'd surmised.

She watched calmly as the hatch clicked open for the Koratan agent and he hurriedly went inside. She pulled her head back as he looked around just before doing so. Once he was through the hatchway, she moved swiftly on her toes to the door, which he had left open ajar behind him, probably not wanting to risk the sound of it closing.

Heather pushed the hatch open just enough to poke her head in and quickly surveyed the scene. The Koratan agent stood with his back to her, looming over the form of a sleeping Zak Brighton in the room's small bed, a knife raised in his hand and ready to plunge down into the dozing ProSec agent.

Heather hesitated for an instant, remembering what protocol would demand of her here. Hatchetface clearly meant to kill Brighton, not capture or question him. It was sloppy for a professional but allowed her the option to simply let it happen and remove the weak link in her mission's chain. It would be so…easy.

She stepped through the narrow gap in the hatch and shut it loudly behind her. "Honey, I'm back from…" she started, and when Hatchetface whirled in surprise, she lifted one hand to her mouth and stifled a scream, or at least pretended to.

The man's eyes flashed with something approaching annoyance. By the time his look changed to one of suspicion, it was too late for him. The knife was already in Heather's hand, and his was still raised awkwardly above his head to stab Brighton in his bed.

She moved lightning quick, feinting a low stab to the man's kidney, which had him twisting his midsection out of the way as he desperately tried to bring his knife down to block her blow from where it was still held high.

Attempting to both dodge and block simultaneously meant he wasn't thinking about anything else, certainly not about her other hand, the one that wasn't holding a knife. And when the heel of that hand impacted his nose and pushed upward hard toward his brain, it should have killed him. As it was, his mad twist to escape her knife threw off her aim just enough that her blow was slightly off-center and only broke his nose.

Hatchetface was still game, and he leapt at her, not giving her time to take advantage of the tears rushing to his eyes from the broken nose, swinging wildly with his knife as if he hoped to overwhelm her by the sheer frantic unpredictability of his movements.

She was chagrined that it almost worked, barely getting out of the way of one of his mad swings as the knife still managed to burn a cut across her upper arm. Still, the surprise of his strategy only lasted for an instant, and Heather was about to deliver a killing slash to his neck when Zak Brighton chose that exact moment to tackle the Koratan from behind.

The move shoved the enemy agent squarely into Heather and sandwiched her in the small space between his body and the closed hatch. The weight of both men slamming into her was enough to force the air out of her lungs and cause her to drop her knife to the cabin floor. Then, abruptly, the weight was gone as Hatchetface pushed off her and turned to face his new attacker.

The knife took Brighton in the shoulder, and he howled in pain, twisting away by instinct and wrenching the weapon out of the Koratan's hand. Heather fought not to swear loudly —first-class cabins on starliners were supposed to be entirely soundproofed, but she wasn't ready to trust her life to what the advertisements said. But instead of cursing her luck, she leapt forward and grabbed Hatchetface from behind, locking her forearm around his neck.

He struggled mightily, trying first to reach out and withdraw the knife from Brighton's shoulder but then abandoned that when the ProSec analyst jerked backward and fell onto the bed, taking the knife with him. Then one of Hatchetface's hands went to grab Heather's arm around his neck while he used the other elbow to lash out behind him and hit her in the side.

Kilgore grunted at the impact but didn't loosen her death grip. The Koratan backed up quickly, taking her with him and slamming her against the hatch as he inadvertently had before. As before, it knocked the wind out of her, but she still didn't loosen her grip on the man. She was the better fighter and could move faster than the enemy agent, but in the small space, he would be able to corner her eventually and use his superior strength to his advantage, so she knew that releasing her grip on him now could easily mean her death.

Slowly, inexorably, Hatchetface's struggles slowed, and he sank to his hands and knees, and then his stomach as Heather's weight on his back pushed him down. A few moments after that, all his movements stopped.

Heather held on for another full minute to make sure the man wasn't faking. Finally satisfied that he'd passed out from the lack of oxygen to his brain, she released her chokehold and stood up to survey Brighton and the room.

The room was a disaster. The manner of the Koratan agent's death luckily meant there wasn't a ton of blood on the deck or the bulkheads, but there was enough from where he'd stabbed her and from where she'd broken his nose. Brighton's shoulder wound was also bleeding onto the bed sheets, the red bright against their off-white color.

Brighton himself was whiter than the sheets, though a quick glance at the knife in his shoulder showed her it wasn't a serious injury. In the Koratan agent's haste in fighting two opponents, he'd hit Brighton's collarbone, which had deflected and slowed the blade enough that it had only sunk in a few centimeters into mostly muscle. But to look at the ProSec analyst's face, he clearly thought he was about to die.

"That," she said to him with a hard edge in her tone, "was monumentally stupid. I should have let him kill you."

Brighton, whose face had already lost all its color, looked at her with wide eyes and didn't respond, though his mouth worked silently as if he were pantomiming speech. She shook her head in dismay.

"You may have just ruined this entire mission, you idiot."

For a fleeting moment, something passed across Zak Brighton's face that almost looked like...hope? "The—then you'll have to abort the mission?" he stammered, and this time, she could definitely hear the hope in his tone. The little fight and his minor stabbing had obviously unnerved the desk jockey analyst enough that he was likely having all sorts of second thoughts about being her backup on this mission, orders or not.

"No," she said, recognizing as she did so that she actually shared a sliver of the ProSec man's hope. "We can still salvage this if we work quickly."

Brighton frowned and nodded dumbly in reply as he sat up—wincing from the pain of the knife still in his shoulder—

and looked down at the unconscious Koratan agent. "What do we do with him?"

"We kill him and space the body," she answered simply, causing him to frown more.

He actually seemed squeamish at the thought, which was odd for a ProSec agent, even for an analyst. The Promethean Security Service wasn't exactly known for its…forbearance in situations like this. In fact, if anything, ProSec agents were usually a little too quick to dispatch their perceived enemies. But Brighton looked as if he'd bitten into a lemon. Maybe he was so used to sitting safely behind a desk and not getting his own hands dirty that he was able to ignore his organization's bloody tendencies.

Still, the obviousness of her response won out, and he didn't argue with her. But he did grunt loudly when Heather pulled the knife out of his shoulder, though at least he didn't scream again. Thus far, no one had come to the cabin to see what might have caused his first screech or any of the other noise, which Heather hoped meant the soundproofing had done its job.

She quickly dressed his wound using a small first aid kit in his cabin's bathroom. Once done, he helped the best he could as they picked up the unconscious enemy's body, and Heather stuck her head out of the hatch to find a blessedly empty passageway, it being the middle of the night by the ship's clock.

It took less than 30 seconds to carry the Koratan agent to the first-class airlock, where Heather's implant made quick work of the rudimentary AI, and they opened the inner hatch and deposited the unconscious Hatchetface inside.

Then, Heather closed the inner door, sealing the agent in the airlock, and commanded the AI to cycle open the outer door without evacuating the air first while suppressing its notification routines so that no one in the ship's cockpit or crew areas would see an alert about the opening airlock. Seconds later, the Koratan agent's body was flying through space perpendicular to the starliner and quickly falling behind the accelerating ship. Whether the enemy agent ever regained consciousness or simply suffered explosive decompression in his sleep was anyone's guess, and she frankly didn't care. At least this way, he was dead and gone.

But there was still the trashed cabin to consider. For that, Heather had a far more elegant and simple plan.

It took only about a minute for the flight attendant to respond to the summons from Brighton's cabin. When the uniformed woman arrived, she stopped in the doorway and put a hand to her mouth in shock.

What she saw was an apologetic-looking Heather holding one of the blood-soaked bed sheets, crumpled up, against Zak Brighton's now-bloody nose. He *really* hadn't liked it when, upon returning to the cabin, she'd punched his nose without warning and caused the bleeding, but she was far beyond caring what the ProSec man did or didn't like. She was cleaning up *his* mess, after all.

"Wha—what happened?" the attendant gasped, looking around at the small blood spatters throughout the cabin.

"He fell in the shower and smacked his face against the sink," Heather said, making her voice higher like a girlfriend in distress. "We mostly got the bleeding stopped, but he made a horrible mess of the room. Do you think we could get some clean sheets and maybe something to clean up the blood?"

The attendant, still open-mouthed, nodded and backed out through the hatch slowly, then hastened off to get what they needed. That the woman hadn't even questioned why Heather was in a first-class cabin rented only to a man traveling alone was a testament to the discretion starliners were famous for.

"You broke my nose!" Brighton yelled—or tried to around the bedsheet covering his face.

"You deserved it," she snapped back at him. "I should have let that guy kill you. It would have saved me the trouble of doing it myself! Besides, it's not broken, you big baby. You'll be fine."

For a moment, he looked at her in horror, like he was unsure if she were about to plunge another knife into him. She shook her head at him, though she didn't smile. "Relax. You get to live…for now. But I'm cutting you loose as soon as we get down on the planet's surface."

He shook his head vigorously so that she had to struggle to keep the pressure on his nose.

"Can't," he mumbled through the sheet. "My orders say to stay with you and help."

Heather looked pointedly around the room. "Like you helped me here? Look, I'm sure you're really good at whatever analyst desk you inhabit in some underground ProSec secret base," she was laying the sarcasm on thick. "But you're so far out of your element here that you may as well be wearing a sign that says 'Promethean agent, come murder me'. I can't afford to keep you with me."

"But…the orders…" he mumbled lamely.

She was about to answer when the hatch opened after a brief knock, and the attendant from before poked her head in. Seeing that nothing had changed, she shouldered the hatch open the rest of the way and brought in a stack of sheets and towels with a spray bottle balanced on top.

Wordlessly and with her nose crinkled up, the attendant started to help Heather clean up the room, unknowingly assisting in destroying evidence of the murder of one of her own star nation's government operatives.

It took about 20 minutes to remove the worst of the blood from the carpet, change the bed sheets, and even wipe off some spatter from the bulkheads. But when they were done, only a small dark stain on the deck remained, which could have been a spilled drink if they hadn't known better.

Heather thanked the woman and ushered her out of the cabin and then turned back to face Brighton.

His nose had stopped bleeding by now, and he was sitting back on the freshly made bed, cotton swabs shoved up his nose, regarding her with another frown. "You can't just ditch me," he said, probably trying to sound resolute but with a noticeable tremor in his voice. "You know what will happen to me if I go back to Promethean space against my orders."

Kilgore frowned right back at him. "And how is that my problem?"

"Well…uh…" he said, suddenly unsure of himself. "You'll be disobeying orders, too, by sending me back."

She shook her head. "Try again. My orders give me a lot of latitude in how I execute my missions. All I have to do is tell my superiors about your monumental screwup here on the ship—I mean, were you even *trying* to be inconspicuous?—and they'll never question me leaving you behind." She chose not to tell him that her superiors would more likely question why she didn't throw him out of the same airlock with the Koratan agent. He already looked like he was on the verge of panic.

"But I can help you. I can!" he argued.

She raised her eyebrows at him. "Really? How?"

He frowned for a moment and she could see him desperately searching for an excuse to convince her to keep him with her, though given how unsuited he was for this type of work, Heather couldn't understand why he wanted to stay. Sure, his superiors would be upset that he didn't execute his orders, but they'd have to recognize that sending an analyst to do a job that would stretch even a senior field agent was pure lunacy on their part.

This reminded her, and she set her implant to running a deeper check of the orders he'd shared with her. A lot about the situation wasn't adding up.

"I know the Koratans really well," he finally said. "I spent six months on Koratas working in the embassy here."

Heather shook her head. "Not good enough. I've spent time in the Confederacy as well, and I didn't need an embassy cover to blend in."

His face fell further. "But do you know Koratas itself? I'm familiar with the capital city."

"It's nothing I can't figure out on my own," she countered. Heather had actually never been to Koratas, the Confederacy's capital world, but she'd rather trust a map on her implant than this idiot's help.

"I've *met* Francisco Ignacio Juarez and his family!" Brighton blurted out next. "At an embassy dinner once. His wife and daughter were there!"

That stopped the retort Heather already had forming on her lips. Not because his knowing the first family would do her any good—a single meeting wouldn't have been enough for him to gain any true insight that wasn't already in her files on the targets—but because she still couldn't figure out why he was trying so *hard* to stay on the mission with her, and his latest attempt had the air of desperation.

Obviously sensing that he wasn't convincing her, he got a look in his eyes that told her he was about to play his trump card. "There are additional details, not in the orders, that you need to know. But I was instructed not to share them until we arrive on Koratas."

Heather regarded him coldly. "I could just torture it out of you, you know? Or hack your implant."

His face went even whiter than it had after his loss of blood, and she could tell that her words had terrified him. Implants, with their complex encryption augmented by organic algorithms based on the unique brain waves of their host, were by all conventional wisdom unhackable. That didn't stop all sorts of rumors from flying around about shadowy government agencies, black hat privateers, or even pirates who had somehow figured out how to hack them anyway. It was a recurring topic of B-list movies. By Brighton's expression, Heather could tell that he was seriously asking himself if the King's Cross might have discovered a way. *She* knew they hadn't—implants remained just as unhackable to her as to anyone else—but she wasn't going to tell *him* that.

Then, he did something unexpected. The fear fled from his face, and he squared his shoulders and stood up from the bed to face her more directly. "Hack me then. But I'll never give up the information I have unless you take me with you."

She regarded him for a few long moments, running through all the angles in her head and hoping that only her cold stare might make him crack. Finally, she shrugged.

"Fine, but you give me a piece of what you know now to prove you have something. Then I'll consider keeping you around as far as Koratas."

He frowned, and, for a moment, she thought she'd successfully called his bluff. Then her implant pinged, and she examined the data he'd sent her, nodding appraisingly as she did so. "So the Koratan Green Party is withdrawing their support for Ignacio Juarez? That's solid intel, I suppose, especially since it hasn't been made public, but I'm not sure how it helps me on my mission."

A new confidence sprung into Brighton's features, and he leaned forward conspiratorially. "It helps because it means that they're not going to let the president speak at their normal pre-election convention. Nor will he be able to visit party headquarters on the night before the vote, as is tradition. Which means he'll need to hold his own rally to get those last-minute votes. And my analysis says he'll do that someplace very public where he can raise his middle finger high to those who think he'll be scared to show his face after the failed invasion. He's got to be worried about what we'll do to retaliate against him, so he'll feel the need to go far out of his way to show us and his people that he's not scared of us."

She shook her head and repeated her earlier statement. "That's a good analysis, but it doesn't really help my mission all that much."

He actually smiled a little. "It does because one of the files on my implant is the standard plans for police and Confed patrol and roadblock patterns for several venues where the president is likely to hold his rally."

Kilgore couldn't help it. Now her eyebrows went up in surprise, and she cocked her head at the man. "Prove it. Share those with me now."

Brighton shook his head vigorously. "And give up one of the only incentives you have to keep me around? No, I'll give them to you when we're on final approach to Koratas and not a moment sooner.

Heather frowned and shook her head, her hand going around to grasp the hilt of the knife strapped in its customary spot on her lower back under her shirt.

TWELVE
BRIGHT COLORS
SPARROW

Sparrow had never visited Novo Recife before and was unsure what to expect when she arrived. The Koratan Confederacy was a large collection of star systems that had originally been settled by people from all over Earth's South American continent, or so she'd been told in school. At some point, several centuries ago, a consortium of some of the richest of those systems had started buying or simply annexing the others until the Confederacy had formed and adopted a republic-style government, though with a far stronger executive branch than most.

But even hundreds of years later, that didn't mean that each and every system and planet had adopted a common culture or even language. Novo Recife was an example of this. The people here, supposedly from a region of Earth known as Brazil, spoke Portuguese and had a unique culture that set them apart from the surrounding worlds. They ate different foods—except for the chain restaurants, of course—listened to mostly different music, and dressed far differently from the rest of the Confederacy.

Sparrow knew all these facts from reading up on the

world, and they were the very reasons she'd felt the King's Cross agent might come through here to detect anyone following them. But a simple reading of the facts didn't prepare her for what greeted her when she stepped off the shuttle next to Wolf at the government port in the planet's capital city of Desembarque.

First, there was the sun. Koratas' primary star was a blue giant, exceedingly rare in human-controlled space and even rarer to host inhabitable worlds. But Novo Recife had a class G yellow star, which she'd read was supposedly the closest to Sol—Earth's sun—of any star in the Confederacy. As she stepped off the shuttle into the warm humidity of Desembarque, she stopped to look up at the star and feel its rays on her face.

It just felt...right. It was odd, really, that it should be so. Sparrow had never even been close to Earth. In fact, she'd only left the Confederacy once on a mission to a neighboring star nation. And lots of inhabited worlds she'd been on orbited yellow stars similar to Sol, but something about the local star here just felt like it was better than any other sun she'd ever been in proximity to.

Maybe that was why the locals called their star Mesmo—it translated to 'same' in English—because it was effectively the same as the star that the early settlers may have still remembered from the old homeworld.

Home! Victoria exulted in her head.

What do you mean by home? You've never even been here, chica, Trina said snidely.

And how would you know, idiota? Victoria snapped back.

Because we share the same brain and body, you tonta. If I've never been here, then neither have you!

Come now, children, Katarina chided in a condescending tone. *Let's not fight about stupid things.*

Well, it still feels like home, Victoria huffed and then

retreated, probably to go take a nap. It was her usual avoidance mechanism.

Sparrow listened to them idly as she studied the city of Desembarque through the windows of the car sent to collect her and Wolf from the government port.

Besides the sun, the next thing that struck her about Novo Recife was the color. Everywhere she looked, the buildings were anything but the uniform earth tones she was used to on Koratas. Here, each edifice seemed to be painted in a color almost calculated to clash with the buildings next to it, but together, they struck an odd sort of harmony that made the entire place just feel more vibrant and alive.

She decided she liked it, as she did the people who inhabited those buildings. Almost everyone she saw on the street was dressed in bright and often riotous colors, often with hats and other headwear and a broad assortment of shoes, though the average person wore sandals in the hot, humid air. Of course, she still saw the occasional business suit, but even these were far less conservative than on other worlds.

It's all so ugly, Katarina complained. *There's no order to any of it. How do people live here?*

I think it's pretty, Trina countered. *There's beauty in the chaos. I love your home, Victoria.*

There was no response from the other woman, and Sparrow searched for her in her head, finding Victoria hunkered down in her usual corner. But Trina's sudden turn from mocking her to complimenting her 'home' had her poking her head out cautiously.

Lola, what do you think? It's pretty, right, chica? Trina asked next, probably trying to poke Katarina a little more.

For a moment, the assassin didn't answer. When she did, her tone was dry and even. *The sightlines…they are all jumbled. It would be challenging to be a sniper here.*

There was a moment of silence before Trina cried triumphantly, *See, Katarina, all of us like it except for you, chica!*

That's not what she said, Katarina started to argue, and Sparrow tried her best to tune them all out, though doing so was a lot harder when she was stressed.

The source of her stress was obvious: Wolf was sitting next to her in the backseat of the car, his eyes out of focus as he interfaced with his implant and ignored the sights of the city around him.

Ten minutes later, they arrived at the outer security gate for the Navy base and were quickly ushered through without so much as an inspection as soon as Wolf pinged his Guard ID to the sentries. When they later arrived at the command center itself, a large building at the center of the base, and were taken to see the commandant, Sparrow had already decided that if she were ever going to live somewhere other than Koratas, she'd like it to be somewhere like Novo Recife.

"Señores," the base commandant, a middle-aged woman who looked trim and fit, greeted them after they entered her office. "I was not aware that the Guard was sending anyone to inspect our base."

The way the woman said it was in the tone of someone who clearly wasn't happy they were there but was going to be just respectful enough not to have it told to her superiors that she had impeded the Guard in any way.

Wolf ignored both her comment and her tone. "We will require a permanent driver while we are here; the one who brought us to the base will suffice. We also require you and your staff to be readily available to us as needed, around the clock, and we require the full assistance of your entire Naval Intelligence staff. We will meet with them in ten minutes in a room you will provide that has no active cameras or listening devices."

He stopped, his cold gaze on the woman, his expression

somewhere between bored and murderous. Still, she didn't wilt under his glare as most would, and Sparrow's estimation of her character went up several ticks. Finally, the commandant nodded. "Will there be anything else?"

Wolf said nothing, but Sparrow raised her hand. "Lunch?" Wolf must have agreed because he didn't contradict her.

The commandant nodded again. "We'll have our intel staff meet you in the North briefing hall, and I will have my adjutant arrange a meal for both of you to be brought there as well. Now, if there is nothing else…"

She let that hang there, eyeing them both expectantly. Sparrow saw a brief tensing of the skin around Wolf's eyes and thought the man would demand more just out of principle, but luckily, he simply stood and walked out of the room, leaving her to scurry after him.

THIRTEEN
MISSION BRIEFING
SPARROW

"You will watch all incoming passengers from all transports that dock anywhere on the planet. If you see anyone you suspect may be a Promethean agent, you will report it here. We have assigned one of the base's AIs to intake your reports and filter and sort them. Your job is not to question whether your suspicion is real; let the AI do that. You will report anything and everyone. Claro?"

Sparrow watched the 36 Naval Intelligence agents and 15 support staff as they took in Wolf's words. They all nodded, though a few looked like they might have questions but were perhaps too intimidated to ask them of the two Guard agents.

"Bueno. Vamanos. Go now and report back what you find."

The 51 men and women filed out of the room quickly and back into the hot night air of Novo Recife, many of them casting glances at Sparrow and Wolf as they did so, but none of them speaking. They were professionals and would do their jobs; Sparrow was sure of that. Whether they would do them *well* was another question entirely. Naval Intelligence hadn't exactly impressed her in her short career.

She was surprised when one of them, a woman probably a couple of years younger than her, stayed behind. The girl waited for the rest of the agents and support staff to leave the small standalone amphitheater the base commander had provided for the briefing and then made her way down to the low stage where the two Guard agents waited.

Sparrow eyed the woman skeptically as she approached, and Wolf frowned in her direction, but neither of them said anything until the young woman—by her uniform, a Naval Intelligence support analyst and a lieutenant—stopped in front of them.

For a moment, none of the three spoke. Then, the lieutenant finally seemed to find her voice. "Uh, sorry, but I thought you should know, señores. One of our agents was due on planet a few hours ago, coming in on a passenger liner. He failed to check in, and the cameras at the orbital never captured him disembarking. It's possible he missed his connection and is coming in on a later transport, but…well, I thought, you know, you said to report anything, even if it's seemingly insignificant."

Despite herself, Sparrow smiled. Even Wolf grunted something that either meant he was impressed or was considering how best to kill the girl. Whereas the rest of the intelligence agents and staff had eschewed much contact with them during and after the meeting, this young lieutenant had been brave enough to bring something to them in person.

Not that it was likely a true lead. With the distances involved in space travel, people missed connections all the time. And since communications between systems traveled only as fast as the ships that carried them, it was quite common that even a government agent wouldn't be able to send word ahead of their missed connection.

But still, it might be something, and it was the first lead they'd gotten, so Sparrow assumed Wolf would have them check it out. "Which ship was he supposed to be on, Lieutenant?" she asked the girl.

"The *Vespucci,* a civilian liner out of Santa Maria IV. The agent, Lieutenant Commander Jaime Muñoz, was returning from a temporary undercover assignment there and traveled only on civilian ships to maintain his cover. Like I said, it's probably nothing, but…"

Sparrow smiled at the girl. "We will check it out. What is your name, Lieutenant?"

The officer looked suddenly scared but swallowed and answered. "Lieutenant Hayley Uvalde, señora. A su servicio."

Wolf interjected himself. "Yes, you are at our service. Until we leave the planet, Lieutenant Uvalde, you report directly to me. You can report to her as well," he motioned toward Sparrow almost as an afterthought.

"Yes, señor. Gracias. I won't let you down," Uvalde said with a quick nod that was equal parts nervous and excited.

"I know you won't because I won't let you," Wolf said, leaving it to the younger woman to catch the double meaning behind his words.

FOURTEEN
OBSERVE AND REPORT

HEATHER KILGORE

"So, what now?" Zak Brighton asked as they got out of the taxi in the middle of Desembarque, the capital city of Novo Recife.

Heather let out a deep breath, questioning for the thirtieth time or more why she'd decided to let the ProSec analyst tag along. It was a stupid decision, even if he had some magic intel in his implant and wasn't simply lying through his teeth about that. But he'd made it clear that if she ditched him, he'd probably just keep trying to follow her anyway. At least this way, she could keep an eye on him. The alternative, however, of just killing the man and dumping his body somewhere was still very much on the table.

But she replied to him anyway. "Now, we find a way into the GNN offices. We download the first lady's schedule, and we get on the next liner to Koratas after that." As she spoke, she surveyed the building in front of them and across the street: Galactic News Network's regional headquarters for this part of Koratan space.

"Just like that, huh?" he replied skeptically. Then, his voice took on an edge of excitement. "Let me guess; we're staking out the building now so you can memorize the security patrol patterns. Then you'll break in tonight, probably by scaling the building or something, crawl through the air vents to the server room, and hack it with your implant. Then head to the roof and shimmy down a drainage pipe and make your escape?"

She turned and looked at him incredulously, unsure if he was serious or not. By the way his face fell at her gaze, she worried he probably had been.

"So, you're *not* memorizing security patrol patterns right now?" he asked sheepishly.

"No," she said, putting her attention back on the building and its front entrance. "I'm watching to see which directions the employees walk when they leave work for the day."

Out of the corner of her eye, she could see his bemused expression. "Why, so you can trail one of them home, knock him on the head, and steal his ID badge?"

She couldn't help it; Heather turned back to him with a scowl. "Listen, *analyst,* you've been watching way too many spy movies. I'm *not* going to knock anyone on the head. Do you know why? Because people tend to remember someone knocking them on the head, or at least they know it's happened when they wake up with a massive knot on their head. The entire point of this exercise is to get the itinerary *without* anyone knowing we have it. So no, we won't be knocking anyone on the head today."

She shook her head at his confused expression and started watching the building again. After a minute or two of blessed silence, Brighton found his voice again.

"So, what *are* you going to do?"

Heather ignored him and kept watching the employees leaving for the day, looking for patterns and indicators that would give her what she needed. Finally satisfied, she started walking down the street in her chosen direction.

Brighton was caught flat-footed by her move and had to jog a few steps to catch her. "Where are we going now?" he asked.

"We're going to find a bar."

FIFTEEN
BODYGUARDS
NANETTE FOURNIER DE IGNACIO

"Señora, one of us has to be with you at all times," the dour woman told Nanette when she tried to go to the bathroom alone!

"Seriously, why do I need Guard agents with me? Is there a threat I should know about?" she demanded.

The woman—she'd introduced herself as Fox, one of those ridiculous codenames the Guard used—gave away nothing, nor did the equally blank-faced man next to her, the one called Raven. He wasn't even *looking* at Nanette during the conversation; his eyes were scanning every doorway in the residential area of the presidential palace as if there might be assassins behind any one of them.

"Is there a threat?" she demanded again. At least the woman had stopped denying she and the man were from the Confederate Guard. Even without the foolish codenames, Nanette could have told that easily just by the way her regular security detail deferred to the two *and* obviously resented them. "Because if there is a threat, I demand that one of you guard my daughter!"

Raven turned and faced her now and shook his head. "I'm

sorry, señora, but our orders are to guard *you*. Your daughter is safe with her regular security team."

Nanette frowned. "Well, I don't believe you. So until you decide to guard my daughter as well as me, I will stay with her so that you will be *forced* to guard her as well."

Neither of the Guard agents replied, which Nanette took to mean they either didn't care or weren't going to argue with her. So she turned heel and stalked down the hall toward Estrella's room, intent on keeping her daughter by her side as much as possible until *someone* cared to explain why two of the most deadly assassins in the Confederacy were assigned to her as bodyguards. Forgotten for the moment was her need to use the restroom.

SIXTEEN
INTELLIGENCE OFFICER

SPARROW

"Report," Wolf's voice came into Sparrow's head via her implant.

"Nada over here, boss," she replied, continuing to scan the faces on the security cameras spread around Desembarque's largest civilian port, many of which were being piped directly into her implant's feed.

Of course, there were so many cameras in the port that there was no possible way she or even an army of helpers could scan all of them, but their new assistant, Haley Uvalde, had had some thoughts on that. She had programmed one of the Naval Intelligence AIs to look for people acting out of the ordinary, flag them, and send only those videos. And unlike most such programs and prompts Sparrow had seen used in the past, Uvalde's algorithm actually seemed to be working. Thus far, they'd managed to tag two drug mules, a woman trying to sneak her cat through security, and a low-level Promethean spy on his way to an embassy assignment—they chose to let all of them go lest they alert their real quarry.

The only thing the AI algorithm hadn't caught was a

King's Cross agent. Regardless, Hayley Uvalde was proving to be surprisingly bright and resourceful.

"Keep looking," Wolf said and then cut the comm connection. He himself was inside the port terminal, watching some of the more promising shuttles disembark in real time while Sparrow and Uvalde were in the car outside with their driver.

Sparrow kept scanning and, five minutes later, pinged Wolf. "I think I have something. There's a man the AI flagged from a couple hours ago. Looks like a foreigner, and he's acting rather oddly."

"Our assassin is a woman," Wolf replied, somehow managing to put a growl into his voice even over the subvocalized implant comms.

He'd dropped that little tidbit on her just a few hours ago, citing unnamed sources within the Guard who had positively confirmed the gender of the agent of the King's Cross who had infiltrated Koratan space.

Don't argue with him, Victoria whimpered from the back of Sparrow's mind. The woman had quickly gotten over her strange physical attraction to Wolf and was now the most terrified of all the voices in Sparrow's head.

"I know, but this guy looks really sketchy, boss," she pressed. "Landed three hours ago and caught a cab toward the city center. Kept looking over his shoulder and seemed to be way too aware of where the various cameras were in the port."

Silence greeted her, and she wondered if Wolf had cut the connection again. When his voice came back to her, she almost jumped. "Was he alone or with anyone?"

Without even being a part of the conversation, Uvalde pinged Sparrow's implant and showed a new video in share mode. Sparrow started narrating to Wolf what she was seeing. "Looks like at one point he was walking with a woman. But the camera never gets a view of her face. Then they separate, and I don't see them getting back together, boss. Still, something tells me she might be our assassin, and he's some sort of backup."

Another long moment of silence. "Did he share the cab with anyone?"

Sparrow repeated the question out loud to Uvalde who interfaced with her own implant for a second and then nodded back at her and pinged something else over.

"Cab records show two people, but the camera blanked out. But get this, it dropped them off in front of GNN headquarters," Sparrow said on her implant comm.

The first time Hayley Uvalde had realized Sparrow and Wolf were able to talk to each other via direct implant connection across the city, she'd been amazed. Most implants had a small direct connection radius—no more than a few hundred meters at most. It had long been thought that any more powerful transmitter buried inside a person's skull would put the brain at unnecessary risk, especially when few people ever found themselves more than a few meters from an Internet access point, and most carried more powerful handheld comms anyway. In fact, there was plenty of evidence that suggested there were some truly scary health risks of having implant transmitters with the power the Guard built into theirs, but the organization always put the mission ahead of its agents' health, and Sparrow had to admit it was rather handy to be able to talk directly to other agents at a distance without risking a signal on public channels.

This time, Wolf only seemed to consider Sparrow's comment for a short instant. "Get down there. I'll meet you as quickly as I can, but if they're that many hours ahead of us, we need to move fast." Then he cut the connection.

Sparrow looked over at Uvalde and smiled; the young woman smiled back at her eagerly. "We get to go?" she asked.

I like this chica, Trina said. *She's eager.*

Sparrow nodded. "Lieutenant," she said wryly. "How'd you like to help me do some hunting?"

SEVENTEEN
THE NEWS BUREAU

HEATHER KILGORE

"For the record, I hate this plan," Zak Brighton said in Heather's implant as they walked into the posh bar two blocks from the GNN building. On the way, Heather had stopped in a public restroom and changed her clothes from her ever-present duffel bag. Now, instead of the comfortable pants and t-shirt she'd arrived on planet wearing, she had put on a silk blouse and a pair of slacks along with high heels. It changed her entire look. She'd also put on some light makeup and let her dyed-black hair down so that it cascaded across her shoulders.

"For the record," she subvocalized back to Brighton's implant, "I don't care. Just do as you're told, remember?"

He didn't respond to that, but from the look he flashed her, she could see he definitely wasn't happy. But she'd been telling the truth: she didn't care, not one bit.

The bar they'd just entered was exactly what Heather had hoped for. After observing several of the departing GNN staffers heading in the same direction, she'd trailed a few of them here. Now that she and Brighton were inside, she could see that it was filled to bursting with harried-looking professionals, including several that she'd seen leaving the GNN building.

She led Brighton to the bar, and they ordered two drinks that they then pretended to sip but didn't really drink. Still, it allowed them to both look over their glasses at the other bar patrons. She caught a few of them, mostly male, eying her. A few more, mostly female, looked Brighton up and down. The man *was* good-looking, even Heather had to admit, which wasn't a bad thing for this particular part of their plan. Of course, he ruined the effect every time he opened his mouth or looked around too guiltily as if he were trying to broadcast to everyone that he was a spy.

"The third booth from the left," she transmitted to his implant, wincing as he cast a far too obvious glance in the indicated direction. Luckily, no one at the booth in question seemed to notice.

The three men there were all older than Heather, but not by much. Only one of them, from her vantage point, had a wedding ring. And by the way the other two were surveying every woman in the bar, herself included, they were likely single.

All of this she'd taken in with just a few glances at the table, but what had really caught her eye was the badge one of the single guys wore on his belt. Even from a distance, she recognized it as the entry ID badge for the Galactic News Network office building.

She watched for a few more long minutes, waiting for an opening and hoping that the three men wouldn't finish their drinks and leave before she got the opportunity she needed. Finally, a quartet of women started to leave a table next to the booth where the three men sat, and Heather led Brighton quickly across the room to claim the vacated table almost before the previous owners could finish gathering their things.

The three men looked up at them as they approached, the married one giving her only a glance but the two single ones spending a little extra time studying her from head to toe before each looking at Brighton and showing flashes of disappointment. She sat where she could see them but studiously didn't look their way. The ProSec agent sat to her right, profile-on to the three men in the booth.

For a few minutes, they did nothing more than nurse their drinks. Then Heather pinged Brighton's implant. "Do it," she said simply.

He grimaced but pinged her back silently. "Are you sure?"

"Do. It. Now," she pinged back, trying to convey her frustration to him without the benefit of actually speaking.

He winced again but dutifully reached out a hand under the table and placed it high up on her inner thigh.

Heather fought the urge to smile at Brighton's uncomfortable expression, and then she slapped him.

The ProSec agent's surprise was genuine; she hadn't shared this part of the plan with him, specifically because he needed to look as shocked as he did now. He sputtered, turning red, and Heather stood up. "I told you I'm not that kind of girl!" she growled at him, drawing the gazes of several of the bar's closest patrons, including all three of the men in the booth next to them.

Brighton sighed and stood up. "Come on, baby!" he said loudly in a tone that didn't fit the words but was close enough. "I bought the drinks; now it's time to pay up." Then he reached out and grabbed her by the wrist.

"Leave me alone!" Heather made a great show of trying to struggle against his grip, and then a hand tapped Brighton on the shoulder from behind.

The ProSec man let Heather go and whirled, looking passably angry as he did so, to face one of the single reporters from the booth. "What?" he demanded.

"She said to leave her alone, amigo," the man said in accented English. "So why don't you go?"

"Or what?" Brighton demanded, and for a moment, Heather thought the other man, who was shorter than the ProSec analyst, might back down. But he squared his shoulders and glared back at the taller man.

"Or we show you what we do to mulherengos here on Novo Recife, tourist!" he said, puffing out his chest as far as it would go. He looked so adorably stern that Heather had to fight not to laugh.

Brighton flashed another look of convincing anger but then slumped in surrender. "Fine. She's not worth it anyway!" He turned back to Heather. "Don't call me." Then he stormed away and out of the bar.

Heather watched his retreating back only for an instant before she turned her gaze to her earnest rescuer. "Thank you so much," she said. "Ah, oh-bree-gad-ooh."

The man smiled at her poor pronunciation of the Portuguese word for 'thank you' and turned to make sure that Brighton had truly left the bar. Then he turned back. "I'm sorry you had to go through that, senhorita…"

"Candace," she said, extending a hand to him. "And thank you for saving me from that guy. That's the last time I meet someone from an online dating site. Can you believe he wanted to sleep with me after only a few drinks?"

The man looked her up and down in a way he probably thought was surreptitious. "Some men are pigs," he said as he did so.

"How can I repay you?" she asked, reaching out and lightly grasping his elbow with both hands. "Will you join me for a drink?"

With a glance back at his two buddies, who both smiled and nodded to him, the short man took the offered seat at Heather's table. She ordered them a round of the local cachaça, a potent drink distilled from sugar cane.

They talked about inane things and drank a few rounds until even Heather's implant was struggling to counteract the effects of the alcohol. Finally, the man worked up his courage and started to scoot his chair closer to hers. Within a few minutes after that, his hand was resting very near to where Brighton had put his before she'd slapped him. Except in this case, Heather pretended to invite and even encourage the contact. It made it so much easier for her to smoothly lift the man's GNN ID from his belt.

Ten minutes later, just as he was starting to get a little *too* friendly, she made an excuse about needing to meet some friends from work at another bar and excused herself. At first, she was worried her would-be rescuer would argue, but he seemed placated by the fake comm code she gave him and her promise to message him later so they could meet up when she was done with her friends.

Two minutes after that, she left the bar and turned right, heading back toward the GNN building. As she passed the open mouth of an alley, Zak Brighton fell into step beside her.

"A little warning next time would be nice," he said sullenly as he pointedly rubbed his cheek.

"I needed you to act surprised," she explained briefly.

"Well, mission accomplished. You get it?"

She nodded but didn't take the ID out of her small purse. Brighton already had their things, including her duffel and his own rolling suitcase. She'd almost made him leave that behind but didn't want to deal with him having only a single change of clothes.

"What do you want me to do while you go inside?" he asked next.

"Keep an eye on the building and try not to be obvious about it."

She left him there, lounging against a parked car where he hopefully wouldn't stand out too much, and crossed the street to the GNN building, walking briskly. Without any hesitation, she walked through the building's front door. From observing it earlier, she already knew the general layout, and she also knew that the security guard spent a lot of time playing games on his implant. So maybe she really *had* been studying the patterns of building security earlier, as Brighton had thought. But she wasn't going to tell *him* that.

As expected, the security guard barely looked up from his game as she walked across the lobby, only briefly checking to see she had her stolen badge displayed but not looking close enough to see another person's photo on it. News was a 24-hour business, so even after normal hours, she wasn't alone in the large open space, and she didn't even draw a second glance from anyone as she used the stolen badge to pass the turnstiles and board the elevator.

The interior plans of the GNN building weren't public record, but they also weren't hard to figure out. The news service liked to post vids of its employees talking about upcoming stories or sharing a 'day in the life' as they called it. From those vids and other sources, Heather had gleaned that the server room was on the fourth floor. She did *not* take the lift there now.

Even with her advanced Guard implant, she had no hope of hacking the servers of a corporation like GNN. They were, after all, a galaxy-spanning news service as the name implied. So even though it would be illegal for them to use Inner Rim or even Outer Rim tech way out here in the Fringe, she imagined they fudged that rule a lot. The security on their servers was probably light years beyond anything her implant could handle.

But, as she'd so often learned, security was only as strong as its weakest link. So, instead of taking the elevator to the fourth floor and the server rooms, she took it to the seventh floor and the reporter bullpen.

When she stepped off the lift, it was into a large open area lined with desks that all had their own computer terminals. While it was possible, certainly, to write an article on one's implant, most news services didn't like their reporters walking around with half-written stories and information on confidential sources and documents in their heads, so they required them to store such things on the main servers. Even their desk-based workstations were only supposed to store confidential documents—like a first lady's public appearance itinerary—temporarily or while actively being used. But rules were made to be broken, especially for the busy and self-important.

Luckily, at this hour, the bullpen was largely empty; a few reporters at the desks nearest the elevators were the only ones present. By their look, they were the junior people, here in case a major story broke and mostly just to make comm calls to their superiors so the real news folks could rush in and take the scoop. None of them would recognize *her*, of course, but it never ceased to amaze her how unlikely people are to stop someone who looks sure of herself.

She squared her shoulders and confidently walked toward the other side of the bullpen, toward where the senior reporters would sit. The larger desks with more ornate decorations made it easy to tell. A few of the junior reporters looked up at the clack of her high heels on the hard flooring, but none of them said anything or challenged her.

As she walked, she surreptitiously studied the desks she was approaching. One of them had a picture on it of the Koratan president, Francisco Ignacio Juarez, shaking a man's hand—no doubt the desk's owner. Perfect.

Heather stopped and sat at the desk before she even read the nameplate. Sure enough, Ernesto Cruz, the desk's owner, was one of the senior political reporters for the GNN regional office. She quickly fired up his workstation, her implant easily bypassing its local security and getting her in. If she wanted to access the servers from it, she'd still be unable, but if her hunch was right…

There it was! The idiot had it not only saved to his local drive but also bookmarked for easy access. It took all of two seconds to transfer it to Heather's implant, and she was done. Still, if she left as quickly as she'd arrived, she would likely raise some eyebrows on the other end of the room, so she sat there for a few more minutes, pretending to busily work away.

Four minutes later, when she got up to leave, her implant pinged her with a call marked urgent from Brighton outside. She winced. Her King's Cross implant may have been capable of communicating with his at a distance, but his transmitter was a standard one and he had to use the planet's public Internet to carry his call to her. It was unlikely anyone would be able to find the call record unless they knew right where to look, but she hated even having it there to be found.

"What is it?" she subvocalized as she started to make her way back to the elevators.

"A car just pulled up," he said, the urgency in his voice coming through in the fast clip of his words. Two women got out and walked into the building. One of them stopped and talked with the security guard, and he looked terrified. I'm thinking they're law enforcement of some kind.

Heather swore silently to herself but didn't break her confident stride toward the elevators. One opened almost the instant she pinged it with her implant, and she got inside. But instead of keying the lobby, she instructed the elevator to take her to the roof. It argued, telling her the roof was off limits without authorization…blah…blah…blah. But her implant's AI had a quick conversation with the elevator's very dumb controller and convinced it that not only did Heather have authorization but that she was on her way to the skimmer that would surely be parked on the roof to cover major news events around the city from the air.

After only a second of hesitation, the elevator agreed, and moments later, she stepped out into an enclosed space on the building's roof. She hacked the door controls and then was outside on the roof itself, nine floors above the street.

EIGHTEEN
EMPTY ROOFTOP
SPARROW

Trina was good with people. She barely even had to threaten the security guard before he let her and Hayley Uvalde into the building with access cards that would get them into any secure area. She didn't tell the guy she was Guard, but he still might have peed his pants a little at some of the not-so-subtle implications she made about her status.

Should have just let me handle him, garota, Victoria said. She was awake since Wolf wasn't around right now. Still, they all ignored her. Making the security guard fall in love with them probably would have introduced other complications.

"Server room?" Uvalde asked the obvious question as they got into the lift and started going up.

"No, chica," Sparrow chided. "She's too smart for that. We're going to the bullpen."

It took just 90 seconds to determine that they'd missed their quarry there. Victoria had one of the male junior reporters wrapped around her finger almost instantly. It was a risk to bring the woman out in front of Uvalde, but she hoped the young lieutenant would simply think she was playing a role. He was quick to tell her that, yes, he'd seen her 'friend' arrive and that she'd left just minutes before.

"Go back down to the lobby and watch for anyone leaving," Sparrow instructed Uvalde. "I will go up the roof in case she headed there."

"Why would she go to the roof?" Uvalde asked in confusion as they summoned elevators. "That makes no sense as an escape route, especially if she didn't know we were coming…" Understanding dawned in the other woman's eyes. "She knew we were coming?"

Sparrow winked at her as she boarded the elevator and commanded it to take her up to the roof, unknowingly taking .8 more seconds to hack its controller than Heather Kilgore had just a few minutes ago.

When she arrived on the roof, she surveyed it carefully. It was late Spring on this part of the planet, so the days were long, and it was still light enough to see at this late hour. But there were plenty of shadows where someone could be hiding.

If it were me, I'd have some rope with me just in case, Katarina advised.

Even for a building this tall? Trina asked her. *No, thank you, chica. I don't like heights.*

Rumor is the Prometheans have designed a type of spider silk that can hold a lot of weight without taking up a lot of space. It's possible.

Sparrow chewed on that. She'd heard those rumors, of course—Katarina and she shared a pair of ears—but she'd discounted them as another ghost story of the King's Cross. Still, if they were true…

She looked over the edge and mentally shook her head. No matter how compact the rope, she had trouble imagining someone carrying enough to rappel down all ten stories, at least not without being conspicuous about it.

She spent another five minutes searching the roof from end to end before finally admitting defeat. A call down to Uvalde brought similar disappointment. Whoever the mysterious woman was—almost certainly the King's Cross agent they were looking for—she had somehow managed to escape without being caught or even seen. Maybe Katarina had been right about the spider silk.

Sparrow silently took the elevator down to the seventh floor, where Victoria found the helpful young man who had taken such an interest in her before. She got from him every detail he'd seen of the mysterious visitor, including where she sat and what she seemed to be doing. Then she headed to that workstation herself, pulled up its logs, and her heart sank.

Taking a deep breath, she put in a call to Wolf. "Boss, she was here. She got it."

There was a long silence on the other end of the comm. Then the man said in a cold, even voice. "We'll catch her when she tries to leave the planet."

NINETEEN
DOWN THE DRAINPIPE

HEATHER KILGORE

Zak Brighton jumped in surprise when Heather tapped him on the shoulder from behind, where he still leaned against the parked car, watching the GNN building.

"Don't do that!" he snapped in what he might have thought was a harsh whisper but was more like the crack of a whip.

"Shut up and follow me. We've got to get out of here now." Without waiting for him to answer, she started walking quickly down the sidewalk and turned into an alley, with him almost jogging to follow as he dragged his suitcase and shouldered her duffel.

"How did you get down from the roof?" he asked when he caught up to her.

She didn't answer but kept walking until they emerged on the opposite end of the alley on a street parallel to the GNN building.

"Wait!" he said, suddenly sounding excited. "You did it, didn't you?"

Heather closed her eyes and breathed out slowly. Then she

stopped walking and whirled to face him. In his excitement, he almost bumped into her; he was grinning from ear to ear.

"You shimmied down a drainpipe, didn't you?" he asked through his big, stupid smile.

"If I say yes, will you stop talking and move faster?"

If anything, his grin got even wider. "I knew it! I told you. That's so awesome!"

Stupid analyst. Sighing, Heather turned heel and started walking again, letting him jog to catch up.

"I mean, I was half-joking, but you actually did it! What was it like?"

"Cold," she replied dryly. "It was windy up there."

"So cool!" he said, practically skipping next to her in boy-like excitement. What was it about desk jockeys, especially the male ones, that always made them think that near-death experiences were 'cool'? Let him try sliding down a cold, slippery drainpipe for ten stories and see if he still thought it was so cool.

They walked for another four blocks before Heather thought it safe enough to hail a cab. She switched up identities on her implant so that no one could track her using the one she'd arrived on planet with, and she didn't let Brighton interface with the cab so that no one could track his. She also used her implant to hack the cab's controller and blank out all its internal cameras. It was a risk—someone could flag the mere fact that a local taxi had nonfunctioning video feeds—but it was far less of a risk than letting someone see her face.

Fifteen minutes later, the cab let them out two blocks from the same port they'd arrived through. Brighton hopped out and started to walk in that direction, but Heather caught his arm and practically forced him down an alley away from the port and onto another busy street, where she hailed a new cab with *another* identity and another hack to blank out the cameras, and had it take them toward the opposite side of Desembarque's urban center.

TWENTY
TRACKING THE ENEMY
SPARROW

Sparrow uncharacteristically swore loudly when they emerged from the building and were out of earshot of the still-terrified security guard. They'd just spent ten fruitless minutes interrogating him and checking all of the video feeds inside the building; there were few of them, and their mysterious enemy had managed to hide her face and most of the rest of her from all of them.

"I'm sorry," Lieutenant Uvalde said quickly. "Maybe she got by me in the lobby."

Frowning, Sparrow turned to regard the other woman. "No, chica, she got by me. Give yourself some credit. You did well today; we wouldn't have even known where to look without you."

She shrugged. "Besides, my boss is right; we'll get them at one of the ports. We have a better description now." And they did, sort of. From the memory of the junior reporter Victoria had gently and flirtatiously interrogated, they had a rough height and build and hair color—though black hair wasn't exactly helpful on a planet where nearly everyone was of Brazilian descent.

"Well, we know that they're using cabs to get around, right?" Uvalde said quickly.

"Sí, chica. But an enemy agent is going to know to use a fake ID and probably scramble the video feed as well."

"Exactly!" Uvalde said. "And I just checked the server logs for all the local cab companies, focusing on their bug reports."

Sparrow stopped and looked at the other woman with a raised eyebrow. "You can do that? So quickly?"

Uvalde blushed. "Well, not legally. But I have some backdoors I've used to track a few people of interest across the city before."

Sparrow pursed her lips and nodded appreciatively; even with her Guard overrides, it would have taken her a few minutes to replicate the feat. "So, anything from it?"

The intelligence analyst perked up. "Yes! There was a cab that picked up two people a few blocks from here and took them toward the North Port. Dropped them off a couple of blocks away from it, probably so they could hide their exact destination. But it's pretty obvious, especially since the cab reported a bug with its video feeds...one that mysteriously corrected itself as soon as its passengers disembarked."

"Yes," Sparrow said thoughtfully. "Maybe a little too obvious, but it's possible they thought we wouldn't pick up on it."

She put in a call to Wolf and shared the intel with him. He agreed with her that it seemed too easy but immediately ordered a dozen of their coopted agents to converge on the North Port just in case.

"Are we headed to the port?" Uvalde asked her anxiously when she ended the call with Wolf.

Sparrow shook her head. "No, we are going in the opposite direction. Tell me, there is a small shuttle station on the city's southern edge. What is it used for?"

TWENTY-ONE
CARGO SHUTTLE

HEATHER KILGORE

"That's an automated cargo shuttle," Zak Brighton said with no small amount of trepidation as Heather led him through the shadows of the small cargo field on Desembarque's southern outskirts. "It doesn't even have life support."

"It won't matter if you don't stop talking. What part of 'stealth' do you not understand?" she hissed back, shutting him up…finally!

He'd saved her by spotting the two enemy agents—though of what agency was unclear—entering the GNN building, thereby proving that it was useful to have a second person on a complex mission like this one…sometimes. Other times, he just got in her way—pretty much *every* other time thus far.

Still, she knew it was only a matter of time before whoever was pursuing them found evidence of him being with her, whether from port cameras or taxi records or by tracking down the reporter whose ID she'd stolen and used to enter the GNN offices. If she ditched Brighton now, he'd be captured quickly and would give their enemies a wealth of intel, effectively forcing her to scrap the mission.

Heather almost stopped to consider that. After all, she *really* thought this mission was a bad idea. And if she was being honest with herself, she *really* didn't want to complete it. So maybe the best thing to do would be to *let* Brighton get captured so she would have to abort and head back to Promethean space. It would be the perfect out and one that not even her superiors would argue with; they'd be so busy reaming ProSec for sending an analyst of all people to support her that they wouldn't even stop to think that maybe she had had a hand in...

She shook off the thought. Zak Brighton may be annoying and incompetent, but he was still trying to help her. The King's Cross may have taught her to ruthlessly use anyone she needed to in order to achieve her ends, but she'd broken that rule pretty quickly with the farm boy on Hudson, Jimmy O'Neal. In doing so, she'd discovered that she had a soft spot for people who only wanted to help her. Brighton was an idiot, but he *wanted* to be helpful.

He didn't talk—blessedly!—the rest of the way to the cargo shuttle, and she led him onboard and into the hold. There, behind a stack of crates, she found what she knew would be there. There were still port workers around, overseeing the loading of the shuttle's cargo, bound for one of the orbitals above, so she used hand gestures to make Brighton understand the plan. A few minutes later, they were both decked out in the emergency vacsuits they'd found hung on one of the bulkheads, and they had crammed themselves between two stacks of crates so close to each other that no one would suspect two human beings could, much less would, choose to hide between them.

They were still there when the cargo bay doors closed,

plunging them into darkness lit only by dim red emergency lamps. Then, they felt the rumble of the shuttle's massive engines as it lifted off the planet.

TWENTY-TWO
THE PORT
SPARROW

"Where are those three shuttles going?" Sparrow asked Hayley Uvalde as they arrived at the small cargo port and watched the fiery trails of three different shuttles lifting higher in Novo Recife's atmosphere.

"I don't know," the Naval Intelligence officer answered, drawing a sharp look from Sparrow. Sheepishly, the young woman shrugged. "I don't have a backdoor into this port, but I can hack it if you'll give me some time."

Sparrow frowned. "No, chica. We'll just go ask port administration." Then, reluctantly and recognizing she was already taking way too many risks around the Naval Intelligence officer, she let Katarina take control. Port administrators loved numbers, plans, and spreadsheets. So did Katarina. She'd get them to give the information she needed, but it would take a few minutes that they didn't have to waste.

TWENTY-THREE
DINNER PREPARATIONS
NANETTE FOURNIER DE IGNACIO

Nanette studied her face in the mirror, doing her best to ignore the stern Guard agent behind her.

Nanette was supposed to accompany her husband tonight to a dinner with the speaker of the house. It was a last-ditch attempt to convince the woman not to formally withdraw the party's support for his reelection. There was no way it would work; even Francisco had to know that, but he would be extremely upset if his wife showed up with the marks of his earlier handiwork on her face. So right now, she was trying to cover up the still healing cut beneath her eye, not to mention the giant black eye above it, with copious amounts of makeup.

"One of you needs to stay here with my daughter," she said sternly as she did so. The agent, Fox, didn't even twitch. "Seriously, I won't go unless one of you stays behind with Estrella to protect her."

"Señora, your daughter is not at risk. You are. And we cannot—"

"I. Won't. Go." She said, biting off each word. "And you

can explain to my husband why his wife isn't at an important dinner."

The Guard agent frowned but then, to Nanette's extreme relief, didn't call her bluff. Instead, she nodded. "Raven will accompany you, and I will stay behind with your daughter."

"Thank you," Nanette said in genuine gratitude and went back to trying to hide the purple bruise surrounding her eye.

TWENTY-FOUR
THE TRAMP FREIGHTER

HEATHER KILGORE

The tramp freighter looked much like any other across the galaxy. Even when viewed only partially through station viewports, it appeared to be on its last legs, like it was being held together with duct tape and the sheer stubbornness of its crew.

Next to all of the other freighters in the Iguape Orbital above Novo Recife's southern hemisphere, the tramp freighter was almost negligibly tiny. It was a StarHauler 3200, a class of ship that Heather had actually ridden on once, though it wasn't a fond memory. But that made it even more attractive to her now, as the 3200 was famous for being able to operate with a very small crew. At most, there might be six spacers on board, and that was more than she would have liked but far less than would have presented her with a threat.

"Try to look intimidating," she instructed Brighton as she finished hacking the StarHauler's inner airlock door. She had her knife but had ditched the gun she'd acquired on Santa Maria IV to get through customs here at Novo Recife and hadn't had a chance to secure a new one. "And if it turns into a fight, stay out of my way. Got it?"

He gulped next to her but said nothing as the airlock hatch swung open, revealing a corridor inside that very much matched the ship's decrepit exterior. She started moving, creeping quickly but relatively quietly through the ship's corridors, wincing internally every time Zak's big feet made too much noise on the metal deck.

It took only 30 seconds before they encountered the first crewmember. It was a woman standing at a console outside the cargo bay, probably checking the bay's temperature and pressure readings before undocking procedures started. She turned at the sound of Brighton approaching behind Heather but was out cold from Kilgore's blow to her temple before she could so much as scream in distress.

Two minutes later, after hiding the unconscious woman in a storage closet, they arrived at the freighter's cockpit without encountering any more of its crew. Heather peeked around the corner into the hatchway and spied two people, a woman and a man, going through preflight checks. She signaled to Brighton to stay put in the corridor and then moved stealthily into the small space, turning on her implant's jamming field as she went to keep them from calling for help.

The woman in the pilot's seat yelped in shock as she felt the cold edge of Heather's knife at her throat.

"Either of you move, and she dies," Heather hissed.

Of course, they didn't listen. The woman squirmed and tried to push the hand with the knife away while the man made to move for something underneath the console in front of him, probably a hidden pistol.

Heather put an end to the woman's struggles by letting the knife cut just a little bit into her throat, making the pilot go stock-still in terror. With her other hand, she reached out and clubbed the man in the copilot's seat hard in the temple, hard enough to stun him but not knock him out.

"Get in here," she called back to Brighton. "And seal the hatch behind you."

He did as instructed, and Heather leaned down to speak to the scared and bleeding pilot. "We're not going to hurt you or anyone on your crew. But only if you do what we say."

"Não entendo," the woman protested. "Não falo inglês."

Heather sighed. "Duvido seriamente que um capitão de cargueiro não fale pelo menos um pouco de inglês." 'I seriously doubt a freighter captain doesn't speak at least a little English.'

The woman slumped a bit in her grip but then straightened with another yelp as the movement made the knife dig into the soft skin of her throat again. "OK, fine, I speak English. What do you want?"

"Simple," Heather said. "I want a way out of this system. You're going to take us to the Heraldo jump point, and then we'll tell you where to go from there."

"But my flight plan isn't for Heraldo. The system patrol will stop us," the woman argued.

Heather sighed again. "You get to lie to me once without consequences, Captain. A second time, and I'll make you regret it. Entende?"

"Fine. But I need my copilot to undock the ship."

"Jose," Heather said to Brighton, using the fake name they'd agreed on before boarding the freighter. "Make this guy move and sit at the copilot's station and do whatever the captain tells you. But reach under that console first and get the pistol they have hidden there."

She could almost feel the other woman's disappointment at Heather calling her bluff. But she had to admit the captain was efficient. Five minutes later, she had them undocked from the station and outbound to the Heraldo jump point. It helped, of course, that the ship was already slated to leave at this time; the crew had been readying her for departure even before Heather had commandeered it.

As they went, Heather interrogated the woman, learning that there were only two other members of her crew—an engineer and a cook—whom Heather and Brighton hadn't already encountered. Once the ship was far enough away from the orbital to engage the autopilot, Heather had her implant use a manufacturer's code to lock down the ship's comm and then ordered the captain to have the crew meet in the galley immediately.

There, the crew of the *MV Urso Dançante* met their new employers for this little trip.

The captain's name was Isabela Cardoso. Her first mate, the copilot nursing a sore head, was Fernando Flores. The other woman with a sore head was the cargo master, Lisa Porter, from one of the confederacy's few non-Latino systems. The engineer was a gruff old man named Azevedo—he refused to share his first name—and the cook was his girlfriend, who staunchly refused to share *any* name. The older couple was so stubborn that Heather quickly gave up trying to learn much more about them; it wasn't a battle worth fighting.

"You could have just hired us, you know," Captain Cardoso said with a scowl after Heather finished questioning all of them. "We take passengers sometimes."

"Frankly, I can't have anyone know we're on board," Heather admitted. It was a truth but an obvious one, and she lost nothing by sharing it. Protocol demanded that she kill every one of the crew after they got her to her destination anyway so that no one could talk about her or her mission. It was the other main reason she'd chosen one of the ships with the smallest crews docked at the orbital.

Of course, she wasn't going to tell *them* that. They had to hope that they might survive until the very last moment, or they would never do what she needed them to do .

"And where are we taking you after Heraldo?" Cardoso demanded; the rest of the crew was clearly willing to let their captain be their spokesman with their unwelcome guests.

"I'll tell you once we're through the jump point. For now, just follow your flight plan to the letter and don't deviate. I'll know if you do. The second a system patrol boat even flinches in our direction, and she dies." She pointed toward the cargo master, who frowned back at her. She hadn't chosen the woman at random; by the body language of the rest of the crew, the co-pilot was clearly sweet on the girl, and the gruff old engineer seemed protective of her, perhaps as a surrogate father. Either way, it gave Heather maximum leverage over at least half the crew to use her in her threat.

"Fine," Cardoso spat out. "But someone will notice when we don't show up at our scheduled cargo drop off."

Heather looked around at the worn galley. Even the bulkheads looked like they'd been leaned on a few too many times. Ships like this little tramp freighter disappeared all the time, if not by pirates, then by simple mechanical breakdowns that just as often killed the crews and set the ships adrift far from any inhabited planet.

"I think I'll take my chances," she said grimly to the captain.

TWENTY-FIVE

THE ENEMY ESCAPES

SPARROW

They had missed their quarry…again! They'd tracked all three shuttles to their destination orbitals and then watched all outbound departures from those orbitals carefully, either blocking them from leaving or having the system patrol 'routinely' stop them on their way out of the system and search them for anyone not on the crew manifest.

But they hadn't accounted fully for how crafty their prey would be. It took even Hayley Uvalde a while to discover that the enemy agents had arrived at the cargo orbital but then taken a short shuttle hop back *down* to the surface of the planet's southern hemisphere, and then from there had caught a shuttle to a different orbital entirely! There, they lost their trail, and it was too late to recall any of the ships leaving the system, assuming they hadn't hopped to a third orbital after that one!

Wolf was angry. It was the first time Sparrow had seen the large, hard man show any extreme emotion. And the way he showed it, by speaking softly through his teeth, scared her more than if he had yelled and thrown things.

"Boss, I'm sure we can track them—" she tried to argue,

but he cut her off, causing even Lola to shy away while Victoria whimpered softly.

"No! We missed them here, but we know where they are going. We'll commandeer a fast Navy courier back to Koratas and beat them there." He turned to Uvalde. "You, Lieutenant, are in this whether you like it or not. You will accompany us back to the capital." With that, he turned and stalked off, probably to go inform the Navy commandant that she would be lending them her fastest courier ship immediately.

Sparrow looked at Uvalde, who had turned stark white. "Don't worry, chica," she said with a forced smile. "He's not all that bad once you get to know him." Neither woman believed the lie.

An hour later, on board the courier ship that was thrusting away from its orbital, Uvalde turned to Sparrow from the seat next to her; Wolf was up in the cockpit 'motivating' the pilot, so they were momentarily alone in the very small passenger area. "Why do you do what you do?" Hayley asked timidly.

The question surprised Sparrow, and she looked up at the younger woman, bringing her eyes back into focus and dismissing the window she'd had opened on her implant. "What do you mean?" she asked cautiously.

The Naval Intelligence officer squirmed a little in her seat but didn't break eye contact. "My entire adult life—not that it's been all that long—I've sat behind a desk and gathered intelligence. I've never even been out in the field. Intellectually, I knew that intelligence would be used by someone, possibly to kill someone else. I've always comforted myself that I was doing it to help my star nation, but it still bothers me sometimes. And you…you're out there…" she trailed off and looked away.

"I'm out there actually killing the enemies of Koratas," Sparrow finished for her with a wan smile.

Uvalde looked back up and nodded. "Sí, I suppose. So, how do you do it?"

Usually, Lola does it with a pistol or a knife, Trina chimed in unhelpfully.

That's not what the girl meant, you idiot! Katarina snapped back, and the two women started arguing loudly in Sparrow's head.

She ignored them the best she could. "It's like you said," she told Uvalde, "the people I kill are enemies of Koratas. So their deaths are in service of something larger than myself."

The lieutenant considered that for a moment and then shrugged. "I suppose that makes sense, but I'm still not sure I could ever do it."

Sparrow smiled sadly. "In my experience, you never know what you can and can't do until you're put in a situation where you have to act." She looked toward the cockpit to make sure Wolf was still there, and the door remained closed. Even so, when she continued, she pitched her voice lower just to be safe.

"My first kill was when I was only 16. I had just joined the Guard, for reasons I won't go into, and they usually don't send trainees on missions, but they needed someone young and innocent looking to send to infiltrate a terrorist cell on Nueva Guadalajara. Their leader ran it like a cult, and he specifically targeted young people because they were impressionable and...disposable for the cause.

"I spent three months in his group, slowly working my way up to meet him, earning the trust of each of his lieutenants and ultimately earning his. Then, my handler contacted me and told me it was time. The cell was planning an attack on a local school, and the Guard wanted me to get close to him and take him out to stop them."

She paused, swallowing and trying to decide how to tell this next part. She couldn't tell Uvalde the truth—not all of it.

To do so would be to let the young woman in on all of her secrets. While she liked the Naval Intelligence officer, she wasn't ready to trust her that far.

"I got close to him one night," she continued.

You got Victoria to convince him we wanted to sleep with him, Trina said in her head.

"When we were alone, I hesitated."

You froze. You had your hand on your knife but couldn't do it.

"But then I thought about the children who would die if I failed."

Even that wasn't enough, chica. Even then, you knew you couldn't kill him.

"So I overcame my fear and hesitation and slit his throat."

You didn't. That was the day we met Lola. She arrived just in time, just as he found the knife and put his hands around your throat to choke the life out of you for betraying him.

"He needed to die, so I knew I was doing the right thing."

You refused to face it, chica. You let Lola have control for a full week so you wouldn't have to feel anything about what you'd done. It almost got us discovered.

"If I had to, I would do it again."

You've never once been able to pull the trigger yourself, chica. That's why you have the rest of us. Left unsaid was that Katarina, Trina, and Victoria had also never killed directly. They all relied on Lola for that part.

Uvalde nodded, oblivious to Trina's narration. "I think I understand. You did it for the greater good."

Sparrow swallowed and nodded, though deep down, she knew that wasn't it at all. Lola didn't care about the reasons for killing a person; it was what she'd been created to do. Sparrow worried about it, but she never allowed herself to do so until after each kill. Even then, she always took solace in the fact that it was Lola, not her, who had actually done the deed.

"Thank you for telling me that," Uvalde said with a small smile. "I appreciate your honesty."

If only the poor chica knew, Trina lamented.

"I...admire you for what you do," the lieutenant said next. "I don't know if I could do it, but working like that for the greater good is why I joined Naval Intelligence. But sometimes I just feel so...yo no sé, useless behind my desk. Like I'm hiding there and failing to do everything I can to help out. Sabes? Maybe I could do more."

Sparrow was opening her mouth to respond when Victoria's voice, fringed with anger, interrupted her train of thought.

Don't you do it! Victoria chastised. *Don't you tell her she should become like us! Don't you dare tell this young menina that she should become like her. The galaxy has enough Lola's in it.*

Taken aback by the woman's vehemence in her head, Sparrow didn't reply to Hayley Uvalde for long enough that the girl started to look worried. Finally, Sparrow opened her mouth. "Never think, Lieutenant, that what you do is not important. Without you, we wouldn't have found those King's Cross agents on Novo Recife; now we know who we are looking for on Koratas. You have done much to help us."

After a moment of consideration, the girl looked mollified and settled back into her seat. "Thank you," she whispered, and the conversation ended.

Except for the one in Sparrow's head, which raged on as Trina and Victoria started arguing about every kill Lola had ever made. Katarina stayed silent; even thinking about the killings made her uncomfortable, even when it was usually her plans that made them possible.

Lola also didn't once interject herself into the conversation, but Sparrow could feel her listening in the back of her mind: listening and feeling...nothing. And that had always terrified Sparrow the most.

TWENTY-SIX
PARTY LOST
NANETTE

"I am sorry, Señor Presidente," the speaker of the house said with a false smile that showed she wasn't sorry about anything, "but I cannot ignore my constituency, and they are demanding accountability for Hudson. You understand, of course."

Francisco Ignacio Juarez gave what appeared to be a genuine smile—he'd always been good at expressing grace even if he'd never once experienced it for real—and nodded to the woman while Nanette and the speaker's husband looked on in silence. "I understand that you will do what you must. But I will ask you again: take the next few days and at least consider the ramifications for our great star nation if we upset things further at this juncture. Admiral Torres' plan to invade Hudson was regrettable, but finding scapegoats and pointing fingers will not make things any better. We must heal our wounded nation together."

Nanette managed not to scoff out loud at her husband's ridiculous words. How dare he blame Juanita Torres for Hudson! The naval flag officer was in on it, for sure, along with some of the local Koratan officials on the Line. But *everyone* knew the ambitious admiral wouldn't use the *restroom* without someone in authority telling her it would further her career. And how could Francisco use the woman as a scapegoat in the same breath as telling the speaker not to use *him* as a scapegoat?

It was transparent political pandering and lies at their worst, and luckily, Nanette could tell the speaker didn't believe a word of it.

"I am sorry, Señor Presidente, but I do not see myself changing my mind on the matter. The party has already made their decision, and we will be going public with it tomorrow morning."

Francisco's eyes flashed with anger. The election was only a week away. By holding their announcement until now, the voters in the most populated core systems closest to the capital would all hear about the sitting president's disenfranchisement by his own party before heading to the polls. But Francisco wouldn't be able to get a meaningful counter-message out in time to do any good.

Of course, it also meant that the Green Party wouldn't be able to replace him in the election, but with the Hudson debacle happening only two months ago, there wasn't really time for anyone to mount a true campaign anyway. The party was in full damage control mode now, and all that mattered was distancing themselves from Nanette's husband.

It made her want to smile, but she knew better.

"Now, if you will excuse us, it is late, and we must be going," the speaker continued.

The woman and her husband exchanged a few more meaningless pleasantries before beating a hasty retreat and leaving Nanette alone with a monster.

For a few minutes, Francisco appeared not even to know that Nanette was still in the dining room with him. He stared sullenly at the plate in front of him, using a fork to move the remains of dessert across it a few times. But then, as if a switch flipped, his face flushed red, and he looked up at his wife.

"What was that?!" he demanded, practically screaming the words. "You did *nothing*! You didn't defend me at all. It's your fault she wouldn't change her mind. You…you…"

The next word out of his mouth was so vulgar it made Nanette's breath catch in her throat. She was still sitting there in shock when the knuckles of the back of Francisco's hand slammed into the side of her face and knocked her out of her chair and onto the carpeted floor. Then, the man's boot flew at her face. Her last conscious thought was that even the cold, terrible Francisco she'd loathed all these years was gone. In his place was a frantic shell of the man…one who had gone completely insane.

TWENTY-SEVEN

THE TRAFFICKERS

HEATHER KILGORE

Two days and three jumps on the *Urso Dançante* was going about as Heather expected, with one exception: she actually found herself beginning to like the freighter's scrappy crew. Maybe it was because she saw in Captain Cardoso what Heather herself might have become if she'd never been sent to prison for killing her stepfather. Regardless, as the journey progressed, she started to doubt she could kill any of them when they got her to her destination.

For a woman raised by assassins to be an assassin—raised to believe the mission, no matter what it was, always came first—it was sobering to now realize that she had lost the hard edge that had allowed her to do her job without remorse. It wasn't even that she was starting to go soft, but more that she was already there, *and* she almost found herself welcoming it, which she simply couldn't understand.

First, she'd let the farm boy, Jimmy O'Neal on Hudson, live, breaking protocol in doing so. Then, she'd even gone so far as to replace the truck she'd stolen from him with a newer model. After that, she'd taken on Zak Brighton, a move that she still thought was crazy. Sure, he'd helped her on the way a bit, but overall, he'd been an absolute disaster. Add to that the fact that she was still plagued by doubts about the mission she was on, and it perhaps shouldn't have surprised her that she was having second thoughts about killing five people she'd just met but who had done nothing wrong other than be easy marks for her to hijack their ship.

Unfortunately, as with so many other things in her life, the decision on whether or not to spare the crew of *Urso Dançante* was taken out of Heather's hands in the most gruesome way possible, with just one day left in the journey.

It started when they were about to enter their last jump point to Koratas in the Engaño system. Heather had just visited the cockpit to make sure that Cardoso still had them on the correct course. She could have used her implant to check that from anywhere on the ship—she had full root access to the ship's AI via her manufacturer codes—but visiting the woman in person tended to help the tramp freighter captain stay…focused.

Now, Kilgore was on her way back to the quarters they'd taken over to wake Brighton so she could catch up on some sleep herself. On the way, she passed Lisa Porter, standing at the same console she'd been at when Heather had first boarded the ship and knocked her out. The woman seemed, as she had been then, to be checking the temperature and pressure readings in the cargo bay.

Heather meant to walk on by and ignore the cargo master; she neither knew nor cared what the ship was hauling. It wasn't germane to her mission, and it gave the crew some semblance of control over their lives to keep that secret from her, so she hadn't even asked. But something in the way the younger woman quickly closed the window she'd been studying when she noticed Heather approaching stopped her.

"Everything OK?" she asked Porter.

The startled woman nodded. "Sure, everything is fine." It

had only taken about a day for the crew to start treating her and Brighton with false civility. It was normal in cases like this. Even putting Stockholm Syndrome aside, people could only handle so much open conflict. So, treating their captors like they weren't hijackers and kidnappers was a coping mechanism for the crew, if nothing else.

"What were you looking at?" Heather pressed while simultaneously using her implant to check on what the cargo master had been studying. To her surprise, it was just a simple page showing the life support readings inside the cargo hold.

But then, as Porter waffled and seemed to be trying to come up with an answer, Heather saw something that caught her attention. The O2 readings were off. So were the CO2 readings. In fact...

"You're moving live cargo."

The words stopped the other woman and put a look of pure panic on her face. Heather took a step closer to her so that their faces were only a few centimeters apart. "Porter, tell me *exactly* what is in your cargo hold."

Then Porter did something that took Heather by surprise. She punched her. It was a wild and desperate punch, thrown from the hip at Kilgore's face in a wide roundhouse, and Heather moved so that it lightly impacted her shoulder instead of her face. Then she knocked the woman out for the second time since coming aboard.

Two minutes later, Heather roused Brighton from a deep sleep a little too roughly. Quickly explaining the situation, she got him to follow her. Outside the cargo bay, she handed him the pistol they'd taken from the cockpit and made him stand guard at the hatch into the hold. Overriding the ship's AI, she broke the hatch's seal and entered, dreading what she would find.

It was worse than she feared.

The first thing that struck her was the smell. It was a mix of sweat and feces that hit her like a solid wall.

Then came the sound. It was almost an animal noise, full of fear and horror.

The sights came next. They were the worst of all.

Before she could react—before she could open her mouth to scream—she heard a cry and a grunt from outside the hatch, back where she'd left Brighton on guard. Then Acevedo, the old engineer, came charging through the hatch, brandishing the pistol and pointing it at her head, his face red with rage.

Heather didn't hesitate; she didn't wait for the man to make any demands or threaten her any further. The knife that appeared in his throat, thrown from Heather's hand without conscious thought, made him drop the pistol and clutch at his severed carotid artery.

Behind him, there was another scream, and the man's girlfriend, the cook, rushed in, her face a rictus of rage and hate. She charged Heather with hands outstretched as claws, and the hard edge of Kilgore's hand to her windpipe put her down next to her dead boyfriend, choking with her throat crushed.

Screams filled the air as the 'cargo' in the hold reacted to the violence, and a hot rage rose up inside of her. She couldn't remember the last time she'd felt so enraged. Heather Kilgore had killed dozens of people in her life, but only once—when her stepfather had tried to rape her and had taken a kitchen knife for his troubles—had she ever killed in such a rage.

Grabbing her knife from the engineer's throat and then barely stopping to make sure an unconscious Zak Brighton was still breathing, she made her way quickly forward to the *Urso Dançante's* cockpit.

Flores, the co-pilot, came rushing out, responding to the screams from the cargo hold. Heather met him with a knife to the gut and left him writhing and bleeding out on the deck behind her. Then she was in the cockpit and facing a frantic Captain Isabela Cardoso.

"They're children!" Heather screamed at the woman who seemed to frantically be trying to put the four cockpit chairs between her and Kilgore and somehow melt into the console behind her. "How can you be shipping children?!"

"You don't know what it's like!" the woman argued, her eyes wide with panic. "It's impossible to make a living for a ship this small. So, sometimes, we haul special cargo. It's not that we want to; it's that we *have* to! You can't—"

Whatever she was going to say next was lost as Heather grabbed her by the throat and practically threw her back into the console, causing a number of alarms and alerts to sound where the captain's body hit the controls. "Children!" Kilgore screamed. "Slaves! And you haul them in their own filth!"

Isabela Cardosa was dead moments later. It was as if Heather blacked out; she couldn't remember the killing blow. She stumbled back out into the corridor, the cockpit alarms screaming behind her, almost tripping over the fast-dying copilot as she went. She only made it a few steps further before she sank down, her back to the corridor bulkhead, sobbing uncontrollably.

Zak Brighton, still rubbing his head from where Acevedo had knocked him out, found her there ten minutes later when her tears had stopped falling, and she stared in comatose shock at the deck in front of her, barely acknowledging his presence.

"You saw?" he choked out.

She only nodded mutely in response.

"Porter is dead, too," he said.

Maybe that should have surprised her. She'd knocked the woman out, but it hadn't been fatal. Heather looked up at Brighton's face and saw the barely contained anger there, and she understood. She reached out a hand and let him pull her to her feet. Then they squared their shoulders and made their way back to the bay and its horrible human cargo.

Neither of them spared another glance or a single tear for the dead crew of the *Urso Dançante*.

TWENTY-EIGHT
NO ANSWERS
SPARROW

"They should have arrived on planet by now," Hayley Uvalde said just low enough for Sparrow to hear but not Wolf, who paced like his namesake animal at the front of the conference room. "Even if they took the long way, they should have been here *days* ago."

Oh, the poor chica is really worried, Trina said. *Say something to comfort her.*

"Unless we missed them," Sparrow whispered back.

Idiota! If you were looking for comforting, that wasn't it, Trina said snidely.

"We couldn't have missed them," Uvalde insisted. "We've watched every passenger liner, every freighter, every ship arriving in the system. We have hundreds of analysts at Naval Intelligence pouring through arrival records, watching for any indication of them. There's no way they got through all that."

Sparrow didn't have the heart to tell the young woman that she could think of over a dozen ways to get around the security measures they'd set to prevent the Promethean agents from infiltrating Koratas. On a planet of 15 billion people, with thousands of ships coming and going on a daily basis, there was simply no possible way to watch *everything*. And if she could think of ways through the cordon, so, undoubtedly, could the King's Cross.

Still, she happened to agree with the intelligence analyst that the Promethean agents still hadn't arrived on Koratas. By now, there should have been *some* indication they were here, even if it was the dead body of their first lady, a worst-case scenario. Raven and Fox had been watching the woman closely, and Wolf had worked with the president's office to cut down Nanette Fournier de Ignacio's public appearances to only the most important ones. Thus far, even at those, there had been absolutely no indication of anything suspicious outside of the usual protesters against her husband.

"Are you hearing me, Sparrow?" a hard voice demanded, and she was startled to find Wolf glaring at her from the front of the room.

"Uh, sí, boss. Sorry. Just thinking."

"Care to enlighten the rest of us?" the man demanded.

Well, time to pretend she had something useful to say. "Just that we shouldn't assume the King's Cross is already on the planet. It's possible they got waylaid somewhere along the way. Or our close brush with them on Novo Recife might have spooked them. Maybe they aborted the mission."

Wolf frowned. "Would *you*, Agent Sparrow, abort the mission just because someone knew you were coming?"

She hesitated before responding. There was a right answer to his question, but it wasn't necessarily the answer the man wanted. "No, boss. The Guard doesn't fail."

He nodded curtly. "So why would we assume the King's Cross is any different? They're on the planet somewhere; we just have to find them. So, take your little pet analyst," he waved dismissively at Uvalde, "and go and get me some answers!"

TWENTY-NINE
THE SIDE TRIP
HEATHER KILGORE

Sparrow and Hayley Uvalde were right. Heather Kilgore and Zak Brighton *weren't* on Koratas yet. Instead, they were two systems over, taking care of two dozen very terrified children.

Heather thought of them all as children, but the oldest was actually 20, closer to her own age than to the youngest of the lot, who was only 11. But every single one of them just seemed so *young*.

It had taken half a day of coaxing to get them to start talking to her and Brighton. Even then, they shied away in fear every time they encountered the two agents on the ship. At least they weren't in the filthy cargo hold anymore. Heather had set them up in the various crew cabins, even though it made them incredibly crowded. She had also insisted that all of them make use of the showers and had done her best to find fitting clothes from the former crew to get them out of the dirty rags she'd found them in. As she did so, they started to trust her, and their story slowly came out.

Fiona Aranda was the 20-year-old and did most of the talking for the others. They were from a smaller system on the borders of Koratan space called Asunción. Six weeks before, a group of men and women had come to their village on the planet's southern continent. At first, the outsiders had acted friendly, offering to pay top dollar for the village's meager crops and trinkets. The villagers had thrown a feast to welcome them, and the outsiders had brought enough alcohol to satiate everyone.

Unfortunately, it had all been a ruse. By the time some of the villagers noticed that the outsiders weren't drinking from the same bottles offered to them, it was too late, and the drugs had already started to take effect. The few still sober adults were quickly overcome, and the outsiders roughly rounded up all of the teenagers and young adults from the village and marched them at gunpoint to their waiting ship.

From there, they'd been transferred from ship to ship, always locked in the cargo holds, and always fed the bare minimum to survive and given no access to basic hygiene. As a result, four of their number had gotten sick and died, with the bodies being left in the hold to rot next to their friends until the next change of ships.

On the way, they'd picked up on a few snippets of conversation from their various captors, enough to know that what awaited them at the end of their journey was, at best, indentured servitude and, at worst...well, something far more sinister. It burned Heather's blood to even think about it. That neither she nor Brighton even stopped to consider helping the children and delaying their oh-so-important mission was testament to how angry both of them were at how the kids had been treated.

Now, they were landing their ship on a planet called Nueva Guadalajara, where they hoped the kids could find some sort of reprieve.

None of them had implants, but Heather searched Cardosa's office and found a few credit chips, which she loaded with as much money as she dared from her King's Cross funds. She'd have to answer for those credits upon her return—the Order wasn't exactly a charitable organization—but she didn't think twice about it.

Once they'd landed, she took Fiona Aranda aside and handed her the credit chips. "I wish we could do more for you," she told the woman honestly. "But it would be dangerous for you to be caught with us. Take these and find a way home if you can. Use commercial liners and stay away from smaller private ships. If you can't afford passage for all of you, send one or two ahead to let your village know you're OK and see if they can supply the funds to bring the rest of you home."

The young woman nodded gratefully and surprised Heather by drawing her into a tight hug. Then, without another word, she walked down the ship's ramp to where the rest of the children were waiting. Heather followed and smiled sadly to see a few of the younger ones hanging onto Zak Brighton like they didn't want to part from him. The ProSec analyst looked equal parts flummoxed and despairing. Both of them knew just how hard it would be moving forward for these kids, but Heather had told Fiona the truth: the kids were safer on their own than with her and Zak.

She stopped herself. When had she started to think of the ProSec man by his first name? He was still almost useless to her; the way he'd allowed Acevedo to knock him out and take the gun was yet another example of just how over his head Zak was on this mission. But they'd bonded more than ever before in the two-and-a-half days since finding the children in the hold, like having a shared mission they *could* complete together somehow made them something approaching…well, not friends, but at least trusted associates.

After more tearful goodbyes, Heather lifted the *Urso Dançante* from the planet's surface and watched the ground fall away beneath her. Then, turning to Brighton, she frowned.

"OK, Zak, it's time to tell me why you're really here because there is absolutely no way the Order *or* ProSec would send an *analyst* on this mission. Time to come clean."

He fidgeted for a moment, refusing to meet her gaze. Then, slowly, he started talking. And Heather's mouth dropped open in shock at his words.

THIRTY
THE FINAL PLAN
SPARROW

"It will be at tomorrow's rally," Wolf told the assembled agents.

They were all there: Sparrow, Uvalde, and even Fox and Raven, who had taken a brief break from guarding the first lady while she remained hunkered down in the presidential palace with double her usual security detail.

"It's the president's last public appearance before the vote tomorrow, and the entire first family will be there. The rally is being televised live across the system, and a recording will be broadcast to the entire Confederacy via the fast courier network. Every major news agency will be in attendance, as will all of the president's staunchest supporters and his fiercest opponents." He didn't say the obvious, that the latter group would far outnumber the former.

"After this comes the vote, and killing the first lady at that point is likely to be irrelevant. So, if the Prometheans are going to strike, it will be now."

He's right, Katarina whispered, as though Wolf might somehow hear her. *The rally is where I'd do it.*

You're only saying that because it's the obvious last opportunity for them to strike, Trina said, but her heart wasn't in the jab.

"Raven, Fox, you will both be next to the first lady as her bodyguards. Sparrow, you will be with them on the stage, scanning the crowd for threats. I will be on overwatch in the building across the way, directing our snipers and counter-snipers."

Logical placements, Katarina said, *though it means we will be reacting instead of hunting the assassins.*

"What about me, sir?" Lieutenant Uvalde said, timidly raising her hand.

Wolf frowned at her. He had never really warmed to the Naval Intelligence analyst but allowed Sparrow to keep her around, given her contributions on Novo Recife. They could all tell his patience with her was wearing thin, and he seemed to irrationally blame her for the fact that they'd still had no sightings of the King's Cross assassin and her mysterious male accomplice.

"You, Lieutenant, will be in a surveillance van nearby. I want you running facial recognition algorithms and watching for anything we may miss."

Aye, the van. The van smells so bad, Trina said sympathetically. *Those techs all sweat so much.*

The one with the glasses is kind of cute, Victoria observed.

Desperate much? Trina said, but as before, the laughter in her voice felt forced.

"Yes, sir," Uvalde replied to Wolf, clearly mollified that she wasn't being excluded from the efforts to protect her first lady.

Wolf scanned the room again, looking hard into each person's eyes until all of them were fidgeting at least a little under his gaze. Even Trina shut up in the face of that stare. "We go in four hours, people. There will be no errors. We will *not* lose the first lady on our watch."

THIRTY-ONE
TAKING THE STAGE
NANETTE

"Four minutes, señora," Nanette's husband's press secretary told her. She had never liked the man; he seemed far too comfortable and even happy spinning her husband's lies from the podium each week. That, and he was too good-looking, so much so that it made painfully obvious the extensive cosmetic work he'd had done.

"Thank you, Pedro," she said regardless. Just because she didn't like the man didn't mean she couldn't be civil toward him. Especially since this would all be over soon.

She'd decided last night, after Francisco had beat her again, that this was her last day with the man. In the morning, she'd take Estrella and go stay with friends in the city. She had a little of her own money, squirreled away over the years, and it would be enough to get her and her daughter home to Nouveau Bourbon. They'd simply need to lie low until Francisco was officially removed from office so that he couldn't use government resources to chase them.

"My daughter?" she asked, turning to the head of her regular security detail, a dour-faced woman named Marta. She was one of the few people in her husband's administration, besides Jonas, whom she really trusted. Marta knew about her plans to leave Francisco and had even agreed to help. She'd simply grown sick of seeing her charge covered with bruises from the hands of her abusive husband.

"She'll enter from the other side of the stage, señora," Marta replied, an edge to her voice that belied her own nerves at her protectee being out in public with the King's Cross out to kill her. The Guard had finally admitted that was why they'd been protecting her in such paranoid fashion, but only after she'd refused to attend the rally if they didn't reveal the truth. "I have three of my best people with her. We will keep your daughter safe."

Nanette frowned. She hated that Estrella wasn't by her side—her mother's instincts practically screaming at her that only *she* could keep the little girl safe—but she had to admit that she didn't want her daughter right next to her where she might get caught in the crossfire in the event of an attempt on her life. So, instead of sitting next to her mother, Estrella would sit with a group of school children whom her husband had invited to join him on the stage—spelling bee winners and the like—because he thought it would make him look more like a man of the people.

"Ready," the press secretary announced, and Marta placed a hand on Nanette's back to guide her out from behind the bullet and laser-proof temporary structure that formed a backdrop to the event stage and toward the short steps leading to the stage itself.

"Francesa is moving," Marta said into her comm, and Nanette resisted the urge to snicker at the nickname. Why give her a codename if it was so painfully obvious who it referred to? She was the *only* woman of French descent in the upper reaches of the Koratan government, so calling her the 'Frenchwoman' was a dead giveaway to anyone listening in.

Her thoughts about the stupid codename dissolved as she

rounded the corner to the cheers of the assembled crowd. At least ten thousand people had packed into the small park in the middle of La Ciudad de Los Arboles, the capital city of both the planet Koratas and the entire Koratan Confederacy. Her husband had chosen the park meaningfully, as it contained a small memorial to spacers lost in a long-ago battle with the Prometheans. He thought reminding people of their war with their neighbor might garner some sympathy for his failed attack against Hudson, but it was a vain hope, in her opinion. It was more likely to simply remind people of the horrible shooting war her husband's action almost started or the national embarrassment caused by the Prometheans learning of the attack and stopping it before it began.

She'd thought to suggest the same to one of Francisco's advisers but had held back. What did she care if her husband lost the vote tomorrow? The truth was, she *needed* him to lose. It was the only way she could leave him and return home to Nouveau Bourbon, her marriage to a now-disgraced former Koratan leader no longer of political expediency to her mother's tiny star nation.

She stopped as she reached the top of the short stairs to the stage and smiled broadly, waiving at the crowd. The cheering grew in volume, and she felt a sinking feeling that her husband's ploy to retain power might just work. Nanette looked across to the other edge of the stage in time to see Estrella climb the steps opposite her, and the crowd's cheering—already louder than she would have thought—seemed to double.

Marta led Nanette to her seat, just to the right of the erected podium, next to the empty seat reserved for Francisco. Then, abruptly, the crowd's exuberance died, only a few scattered cheers almost offset by jeers and boos echoing from the surrounding buildings.

The president had arrived. Nanette looked to see her

husband mounting the stairs to the stage, smiling broadly and waving to the unenthusiastic crowd. They would see no visible negative reaction to their jeers, but she could see the glint of anger in his eyes. At least the crowd's reaction meant that her fears were unfounded; even this last-ditch attempt to garner sympathy would *not* save Francisco's political career.

She smiled at that thought, though the crowd and the others assembled on the stage probably misread it as joyous support for her husband. Either way, Nanette felt happier than she had in some time.

THIRTY-TWO
THE CROWD
SPARROW

Sparrow scanned the crowd carefully from her place, standing rigidly at the corner of the stage. She hated being this visible. As a Guard agent specializing in assassination, not protection, she loathed that so many people could see her face at the moment, even though she knew that most wouldn't even remember what she looked like. Bodyguards were like furniture, unnoticed by most, including the people they were there to protect.

Relax and follow the plan. It's a good plan, Katarina tried to comfort her while Lola did her best to burrow even deeper than usual into the back of Sparrow's brain. She, of all of them, hated being out in the open like this the most.

Still, Sparrow did her job diligently, watching the crowd carefully and using her implant's built-in digital zoom to see much further than most of the assembled citizens would have believed possible. Coupled with her connection to the AI facial recognition algorithms in the surveillance van where Uvalde was ensconced, it made for a powerful combination. Already, she had identified six possible rabble-rousers in the crowd, all of whom had already been quietly removed by the ever-present security forces. *None* of them, however, could possibly be the King's Cross agent she had actually been sent to find, but that didn't mean they posed no threat.

She kept scanning the crowd, fighting not to tug at the starched shirt collar that threatened to choke her. The assassin was out there somewhere, and Nanette Fournier de Ignacio would *not* die so long as Sparrow was here to stop it.

THIRTY-THREE
THE VAN
HEATHER KILGORE

Heather wasn't in the crowd where Sparrow and many others were watching for her. Her presence there would have been far too obvious and would have virtually guaranteed her capture after she took the fateful shot. And for an agent of the King's Cross, being captured was mission failure; there were more secrets in her head than in all of ProSec.

Nor was she waiting high up on any building surrounding the small park. That would also be far too obvious, and the snipers and countersnipers on guard all around the venue would be sure to be watching any window or rooftop with a view of the stage. Movement of any kind there would bring a swift and deadly response and worse, prevent the completion of her mission.

No, Heather was in a more unlikely spot, two blocks away from the park, in the back of a nondescript gray van with counterfeit government plates registered to one of the many Koratan agencies providing security for the president's rally. She rested the sniper rifle—the one she'd guarded so closely in her duffel all these weeks, its parts disguised to look like cosmetic devices—on the back of the rear seat, where she knelt facing out the rear window and sighted in on the distant stage.

Up front, Zak Brighton sat in the driver's seat, working with the *other* device Heather had brought hidden in her duffel. It was hard to determine which of the two was most important today.

The very reason no one would suspect her perch was that it *wasn't* a good one. Though the van sat on a slight rise in relation to the park, the shot she would have to make would barely clear the heads of the assembled crowd before hitting her target. The street itself was crowded with security people, so there was a decent chance someone would walk in front of her just as she pulled the trigger. Everything about the spot was less than ideal, which made it virtually invisible to those trying to stop her.

"Target One and Target Two are both in their seats; the president is beginning his speech," Zak Brighton said to her, his eyes fixed on the screen in front of him, his voice full of distaste.

Target One was Nanette Fournier de Ignacio, and Heather had already sighted in on her. But Target Two was nine-year-old Estrella Ignacio Fournier, and Brighton had made it clear that he had no desire to be part of the little girl's death. She agreed. Regardless, she turned the rifle's scope to sight in on the girl, continuing to take note of the range, wind speed, and elevation. It paid to be ready.

"And the other thing?" she asked Brighton.

"Still nothing. I'll keep searching."

THIRTY-FOUR
ANOTHER EMPTY ROOFTOP

SPARROW

President Ignacio Juarez was not winning over the crowd with his impassioned speech about the Promethean threat, and Sparrow did her best to tune out his words, though Katarina, the only one of them even remotely interested in politics, listened with rapt attention and would probably force them all to sit through a recap later.

Something was wrong. Sparrow had no idea what it was, but there was a gnawing feeling in her gut. Or rather, Trina had the feeling. Katarina felt secure in the plan Wolf had put forth; it covered all the angles, or so she believed. But Trina didn't care about the plan, and she nagged Sparrow. Something, she felt, was definitely off.

Lifting her eyes from the crowd, Sparrow let Lola take over and scan the buildings surrounding the park.

I would take the shot from right there, the assassin whispered, mentally indicating a building off to one side at the intersection of two major boulevards, both of which had been shut down by police for the President's speech. Still, it made sense as it was surrounded by buildings of similar heights, and a sniper on the rooftop could make an escape to any of them with even basic anti-grav tech or even a low-tech zipline gun.

She studied the rooftop in question; something about it bothered her. There was no one up there, so the sniper wasn't there unless they were very well hidden, so…

Non c'è nessuno lassù! There is no one up there! Lola practically screamed in uncharacteristic fervor.

"Wolf," Sparrow quickly took back control and called her boss via her implant. The man pinged back to acknowledge receipt. "There's a problem with the rooftop of building eight," she continued. "Weren't there supposed to be two countersnipers on it?"

"Wait one," the man replied brusquely, so she did. When he came back on the line, his voice was still even. "You're right. Neither of the units assigned there is responding. I'm two minutes from it; I'll go check it out."

"You're two minutes from it, but…" she started before Wolf cut the line.

That wasn't the plan, Katarina said in her head. *Wolf is supposed to be on the 27th floor of building two. That's at least six minutes from the rooftop of building eight, accounting for average lift speeds and time on foot. Something is off!*

That's what I've been saying this entire time! Trina chimed in. *This whole thing stinks, chica.*

Uh oh. When Katarina agreed with Trina on something, that always set off alarm bells for Sparrow. Something was certainly wrong. But what? The empty rooftop would be covered shortly and until then…

"Raven, Fox," she subvocalized. "Shift to cover the sightline from the building eight rooftop." She was actually surprised Wolf hadn't already sent the order himself.

The two other agents, standing next to the first lady's seat, shifted subtly, Fox stepping slightly forward to put her body directly between Nanette Fournier and the rooftop in question. It would also block a small portion of the crowd from seeing the first lady, but that was just too bad.

"Wolf, did you find anything?" she subvocalized next.

No response.

"Wolf? Check in."

Still, nothing, not even an answering ping that might indicate he was receiving but not in a position to talk.

Wrong, all wrong, Trina was repeating over and over again while Katarina was spouting off vectors and a countdown to Wolf's two-minute mark. Lola was deadly quiet, still studying the rooftop through Sparrow's digital zoom for any movement, and Victoria was silent in anticipation or fear.

"Uvalde, do you have a location on Wolf?" Sparrow asked the young lieutenant in the nearby surveillance van.

"Negative," came the almost instant reply. "He hasn't been letting me track his implant."

That wasn't the plan, Katarina insisted, her voice urgent, bordering now on frantic, in Sparrow's head. *He should be following the plan.*

The rooftop is no bene now as a sniper nest; Fox is blocking the view, Lola insisted. *The shot will come from elsewhere. Not even the best sniper could hit the first lady now through Fox's body armor, capisci?*

We're missing something, Trina insisted. *I can feel it, chica.*

'Not even the best sniper could hit the first lady now.' Lola's words played again in Sparrow's head. They were missing something—something big. Something…

THIRTY-FIVE
COUNTDOWN
HEATHER KILGORE

"The speech ends in a minute and a half," Zak said quietly from the driver's seat. "You'll want to take the shot before then. And that other thing, I think I might have found it. Getting into position now."

A small, detached part of her brain acknowledged his words, but she otherwise ignored him. They had already agreed on the timing: toward the end of the speech when the security teams on the stage would be starting to relax because nothing had happened yet. It was simple human nature—no one could be at the highest level of alert for all that long, so they would naturally and subconsciously start to lower their guard as it seemed the speech would end without anything happening.

Heather started to slow her breathing in preparation to take the fateful shot.

THIRTY-SIX
UVALDE'S DECISION
HAYLEY UVALDE

Lieutenant Hayley Uvalde studied the AI's updates as she tried not to stress about the location of Wolf. The man gave her a cold feeling whenever he looked at her, so she tried not to dwell on the fact that he was the only member of the Guard on duty that she *couldn't* see on her map. The rest of them had openly shared their implant tracking codes, but he had declined. At the time, she'd simply thought it was because he didn't like her, but now, with Sparrow's question and the unguarded rooftop, she was beginning to wonder…

One of the van's displays beeped, and she turned her attention to it, looking over one of the techs' shoulders, her brow wrinkling in confusion. That wasn't right…there were no drones on duty there. But the blip was there one second and then gone. Sensor ghost?

She was about to dig in further, but one of the other techs called her over, and she looked at what he was seeing on his display.

"Uh, Sparrow," she called to the Guard agent's implant using the van's comm repeater, all thought of phantom drones gone. "I may have something."

"What is it?" came back the short response, and she imagined she could hear the agent's stress even through the implant comm.

"There's a van with government plates two blocks away. It's probably nothing, but..."

"Tell me!" the agent demanded.

"That van is supposed to be offline for maintenance right now. The logs show it's at the Confed Investigation Bureau's motor pool getting new capacitors. It could just be a record-keeping error."

There was only a momentary pause. "Send a team, now!" This time there was no mistaking the urgency in the subvocalized response.

Uvalde quickly dispatched a team, and her implant map showed four regular police officers converging on the location; they would be there in 48 seconds.

"Still no location on Wolf?" Sparrow asked next.

"Nothing," she replied.

Sparrow cursed and cut the connection.

Hayley looked again at the map. Her van was actually parked right at the base of building eight. She was *so* close; she could be on that empty rooftop in a minute or so. Wolf might get mad if he was already there and securing it, but...

Decision made, she left the van quickly and headed across the sidewalk and into the building.

THIRTY-SEVEN BREATHS

HEATHER KILGORE

Heather let out a long breath and did not inhale again. Her heart rate was so slow it might as well have been stopped altogether, and her target was square in her sights. Calmly, she started to tighten her finger on the sniper rifle's trigger.

THIRTY-EIGHT
THE REALIZATION
SPARROW

Lola, back in control now, couldn't stop looking at the supposedly empty rooftop of building eight. Wolf still hadn't checked in, and he wasn't responding. She was about to send a security team to check it out, even if it might upset the senior agent. She and Sparrow were so worried about the rooftop, in fact, that they'd almost all forgotten about Uvalde's mysterious van the instant the woman had noted it. Besides, that was someone else's problem now.

Still, Fox hadn't moved, and there was no possible way anyone on the rooftop could get a clear line of sight to Nanette Fournier on the stage. Even if they chose to try and shoot through Fox to get to her, the Guard agent's thin but effective body armor under her pantsuit would stop all but a rocket. So why were Katrina, Trina, *and* even Victoria still screaming at her about that blasted rooftop? There was simply no way anyone could shoot the first lady from there, so…

Then, she saw a flash of light from the rooftop of building eight.

Sparrow's breath caught in her throat as understanding

dawned on her. With a monumental effort, she wrested control from Lola, who was reluctant to give it up but finally succumbed. In Sparrow's mind, Katarina, Trina, and Victoria all gasped simultaneously as they saw what she was thinking. *Aye no!* Trina screamed.

Before she'd even processed their reactions, Sparrow was moving, sprinting across the stage toward the hidden sniper's *real* target.

THIRTY-NINE
TAKING THE SHOT
HEATHER KILGORE

Heather's heart beat once, and in the moment between that and the next slow beat, she finished squeezing the trigger. Just as she did so, something occluded her view of the target as another person leapt across her scope's field of view. But it was too late. The gun jolted back hard against her shoulder as the bullet flew through the back window Brighton had opened an instant before. Even as it left the barrel, she knew it would fly true.

She watched anxiously through the scope as the leaping form moved past her target just in time, and the bullet hit its mark.

"We've got company!" Zak yelled from the driver's seat, and she felt the van jolt as he pulled it quickly away from the curb and hit the accelerator. Then, all hell broke loose.

FORTY
GETTING SHOT
SPARROW

Sparrow was halfway across the stage when she saw the flash of light again from the rooftop of building eight. She desperately tried to pour more speed into her mad dash, flinging herself in a leap as she neared her new protectee.

Because in the instant before she began crossing the stage, she had realized something horrible: Nanette Fournier de Ignacio was not the target.

Two bullets arrived before she heard the sound of either shot. One slammed into its intended target's head, killing them instantly. The other...

The other slammed into Sparrow's chest as she threw herself across the stage and in front of the person she now knew was the real target: Estrella Ignacio Fournier.

FORTY-ONE
FLEEING THE SCENE

HEATHER KILGORE

The van bounced hard on its repulsors as Zak threw it up and onto the sidewalk to get around a police road-block, and she lost her visual on the stage, but she'd seen enough.

The stunned officers who flew by Heather's vision outside the side window never even drew their weapons; they hadn't expected a threat to come from *inside* their security cordon. So they were caught flatfooted when the van approached from behind their roadblock. They had even been preparing to move it out of the way to let the vehicle pass before Zak decided not to wait for them.

She couldn't blame him as multiple shots from behind them slammed into the back of her rear seat, one of them tearing all the way through and missing her by centimeters.

Regardless, she allowed herself a smile as Zak drove the van for all it was worth.

FORTY-TWO
DEATH COMES QUICKLY

HAYLEY UVALDE

Hayley flung open the door that led onto the roof of building eight. On the ride up in the lift, she'd fidgeted and tried to will the elevator to go faster. It hadn't worked; she'd still been in the short stairwell between the top floor and the roof access when she'd heard the report of a shot from a high-powered rifle.

"No!" she cried as she pushed the door open and dashed out onto the rooftop, only belatedly remembering to draw the pistol at her hip.

It wouldn't have mattered even had she already had the gun ready. The man was already running across the rooftop toward her and the lone exit, and when he saw her, his rifle snapped to his shoulder. She heard another loud crack and felt his bullet pierce her chest and send her tumbling headlong to the hard and rough surface of the rooftop.

FORTY-THREE
THE BETRAYAL
SPARROW

Sparrow gasped for breath and tried to collect herself as she lay prone on the stage, her entire body in shock from the supersonic bullet that had taken her right in the chest.

The very fact that she was still aware enough to feel the sharp pain there told her that her body armor had done its job. Struggling, she turned over and looked behind her, registering the sound of screams all over the stage and from the crowd as they practically trampled each other to get away from the park.

It was Katarina who gained full awareness first, and the very first thing she saw was President Francisco Ignacio Juarez…or what was left of him. The man's face was just…it was just gone from where the bullet had hit it. Blood was spattered on the men and woman behind him on the stage, one woman clutching a string of now gore-covered pearls and screaming in wide-eyed shock at the president's corpse in front of her. Interestingly enough, the pattern of the blood spatter suggested not a rooftop shot at an angle but a shot from directly in front and almost at the same elevation as the stage.

Trina woke up next, asserting control and shuddering at the scene of the very dead president. Then, she turned and looked closer to where she lay and felt a rush of relief.

Estrella Ignacio Fournier no longer looked like an innocent nine-year-old as she stared in shock at her father's corpse. But the little girl was alive! The bullet intended for her—the one actually fired from the building eight rooftop—had hit Sparrow instead, just as she'd hoped when she'd leapt between Estrella and the flash of the rifle scope she'd seen twice.

"Sparrow?" came a weak voice over her implant's comm, a message relayed through public channels. It was so quiet it took Trina a moment to register it; when she did, she immediately surrendered control to the now fully awake Sparrow.

"Uvalde?" she subvocalized in confusion. "Where are you?"

"Wolf," came the weak reply. "It was Wolf…building… eight…he shot…"

The young woman's voice trailed off, and Sparrow screamed vocally into the comm to get her attention, but to no avail. The Navy Intelligence lieutenant's signal on her implant's map winked out as the woman died and her implant lost power.

Hayley Uvalde was no more.

A rage rose inside Sparrow that was greater than the pain in her chest, and she gritted her teeth as she levered herself up from the stage. Casting a quick glance to see Fox still shielding the first lady and Raven making her way swiftly to her and Estrella—both of the other agents looked shocked and dismayed, and Trina whispered that neither looked like they had expected the attempt on the little girl's life—Sparrow fought her way off the stage, painfully pushing aside screaming and panicking government lackeys as she went.

When her feet met the soft carpet of grass that clothed the

park, she felt a rush of hate-fueled adrenaline that made the pain a distant thing as she slowly accelerated her bruised body into a loping sprint toward the corner where building eight sat.

The plan, it was all a trick, Katarina lamented as she ran.

But why go after the daughter? And why betray us like that? Trina asked bitterly.

I knew that homem was no bom, Victoria said with an unusually hard edge to her voice.

But it was Lola who came to the forefront now and whom Sparrow allowed to take full control, even letting her hair turn white in the process. And Lola only had one, almost gleeful thought:

The Wolf is going to die.

FORTY-FOUR
GOING TO GROUND

HEATHER KILGORE

The van broke down a block later as a lucky shot from one of the Koratan security officers took out the left rear repulsor. Even then, the vehicle dragged itself half a block further, kicking up sparks where the damaged corner scraped against the pavement before its onboard AI put it into an emergency shutdown.

Heather flung open the side door just as Zak opened his driver's door. Together, they sprinted into a nearby alleyway, one that went through to the next avenue. A dead end right now would be catastrophic with the security agents on their tail.

"Stay together or separate?" Brighton asked as she ran behind.

She only thought about it for an instant, knowing she'd be far more likely to make a clean escape without him slowing her down. Plus, the Koratans would waste precious time and resources finding him while she got off planet.

"Together," she told him.

They turned the corner onto the next avenue over, slowing to a walk so as not to draw too much attention.

"There!" Heather called, pointing to a doorway across the street through which an elderly man was entering with an armful of groceries.

They rushed across the road, ignoring the ever-present honking of the almost stopped traffic—the streets around the park, particularly the ones that hadn't been closed, were a nightmare of gridlock at this time of day. Arriving at the apartment building door just as the older man got it unlocked, Heather reached out to hold it open for him.

"Carido," she said in a light voice to Brighton. "Please help this gentleman. Have some manners."

Brighton took the cue, reaching out and taking the groceries from the old man before he could protest. For a moment, it looked like the Koratan would argue with the unwanted help, but then his face broke into a smile.

"Thank you, señor, señorita. So many, they do not help these days."

Heather smiled at the man warmly. "Well, we just moved into the building…" she told him, chatting inanely as the door closed behind them. She glanced behind her to see three out-of-breath police officers emerge from the alley through which they'd come, looking up and down the street in frustration.

She didn't feel relieved. They had evaded their pursuers for a few minutes, but soon the door-to-door searches would begin, and the roadblocks would already be going into place.

After all, President Ignacio Juarez may have been hated by most of his citizens there at the end, but that wouldn't stop any of them from turning in or hunting down the Promethean agents who had killed him. She could only hope that Zak's part of the plan had saved the first daughter from the same fate.

FORTY-FIVE
GOING HUNTING
LOLA

Lola examined the scene on the rooftop with the dispassionate eye of a cold and well-trained assassin. She found the spot where Wolf had set up his rifle and taken the shot, putting her into his headspace and miming the actions until she was sure both that it had been him and that Estrella Ignacio Fournier had been his target all along.

The assassin left the roof's edge and walked over to examine the dead body. Hayley Uvalde had such a large hole in her chest that it was an absolute wonder she'd even lived long enough to warn Sparrow of Wolf's betrayal.

Wolf. Lola had never liked the man, but she'd certainly never considered that he might be a traitor to the president and the Guard. Now, Katarina couldn't stop blabbering about how it all made so much sense: the way he'd arranged them at the event, completely focused on the first lady, dismissing almost out of hand the implication that the president's daughter might also be in danger. In reality, Katarina now suspected that young Estrella Ignacio had been the man's target all along.

Lola didn't really care.

Sparrow, deep down, was stricken and made no move to take control back from Lola. She was hiding, struggling to come to grips both with Wolf's betrayal and the horrible death of Lieutenant Hayley Uvalde. She'd liked the girl. Her quick intelligence and earnest desire to serve her star nation —her very presence on the rooftop was proof enough of both —appealed to her, and Sparrow had even been toying with the idea of suggesting the young lieutenant be recruited into the Guard.

Now, she was dead, and the only thing more infuriating than her death—or at least that should have been more infuriating than her death—was the death of the president himself.

Lola puzzled over that part, scanning the rooftop and shoving Sparrow's consciousness deeper into the recesses of their shared mind. Who had been the second shooter in the mysterious van? A compatriot of Wolf's? Or, more likely, the King's Cross agent they'd been expecting? They'd already gotten the reports of the van fleeing the scene, and the forensic techs were going over it centimeter by centimeter while every police force, government agency, and security service in the city—and half a dozen more flying down from orbit—were setting up hard security checkpoints all around the area to catch the president's assassins.

There were two from the descriptions of the police who had chased and damaged the fleeing van—a man and a woman, matching the descriptions of those they'd almost caught on Novo Recife. Lola knew they likely wouldn't be getting far before they were brought down; she only hoped she'd be the one who got to kill them.

Still, Katarina nagged at her: *The reports said the first lady was the target. Why did the King's Cross shoot the president instead?*

Nothing was adding up, and Katarina was frantically trying to make plans to get some answers while Trina screamed in frustration at the dead body at her feet. Victoria, characteristically, whimpered in the background.

But none of them, without the intercession of Sparrow, were strong enough to take back control. And Lola frankly didn't care why Wolf or the King's Cross agents had done what they did.

Standing on the rooftop next to Hayley Uvalde's body, Lola smiled wickedly. She was finally going to get the chance to fight Wolf and the King's Cross. Killing all three of them in one day would be...sweet, satisfying, fulfilling.

It was time for Lola to go hunting.

FORTY-SIX
THE DRONE
HEATHER KILGORE

Five Weeks Before the Rally

"You need what?"

"You heard me." Heather stared hard across the heavy wooden desk at the short, round form of 'Mr. Jones', Hudson's most feared and in-demand arms dealer, as the other woman stared back at her in disbelief.

"You know, that's not easy to get, even for me," the arms dealer said with a deep frown.

"You work in a drone foundry," Heather pointed out.

Jones shrugged and smiled tightly. "Good point. What I meant was that it's *expensive,* even for me."

Heather said nothing but raised her eyebrows and stared at the rotund woman behind the desk.

"Yeah, I guess the King's Cross can probably afford it," Jones admitted with a shrug and a nod that she used to try to unsuccessfully mask her discomfort at Heather's stare. "But what do you need a fully stealth drone for anyway?"

Again, Heather said nothing but kept her eyes fixed squarely on the arms dealer's until Jones looked away. The truth was, she didn't know how she might use it. But being sent deep into enemy territory to kill two closely protected targets meant she wanted to plan for every eventuality. The stealth drone—small enough to break down and hide in her standard duffel bag—wasn't big enough to actually fire a deadly shot at one or both of her targets—unless it somehow got *really* close to them—but it could help with reconnaissance and possibly provide a distraction to help her get away.

"OK, OK," Jones said with a sigh. "But it's not like we just keep those sitting around in inventory. I'll have to have it built from scratch, which means making sure we have all the raw components on hand, switching over a production line, and a whole mess of other things. I'll need at least until the end of the week."

"You have 48 hours," Heather said evenly.

Jones frowned and she steepled her fingers over her ample belly, as was her habit. Then, she shrugged. "Fine, but that'll *really* cost you."

Kilgore slid an untraceable credit chip across the desk and watched as Jones picked it up and pinged it with her implant. Then, the arms dealer's eyes went wide. "Yeah, that'll cover it. Pickup or delivery?"

Heather allowed herself the first small smile of their meeting. "I'll be back in two days to pick it up."

FORTY-SEVEN
THE TATTOO

HEATHER KILGORE

Two Weeks Before the Rally

"Señorita, you are sure?" The artist in the small studio on Santa Maria IV looked dubiously at Heather. He was older, probably old enough to be her father, and he regarded her with the disapproving expression her own father might have worn in the same situation, assuming he were still alive.

"I am sure, señor," she replied with a certainty she didn't feel.

"The cartel..." he started, looking even more uncomfortable now. "They will kill you if they catch you. They do not take...kindly to those who pretend to be members of their group, sabes?"

"And what makes you think I'm not a member?" Heather asked evenly.

The old man grimaced. "Forgive me, señorita, but you do not seem the type. The cartel," he looked around the room even though they were alone, as if he worried that the cartel might be listening in. "They are cold-blooded killers, you see. And you do not strike me as such."

Heather smiled wanly at the man. If only he knew. "I am sure," she repeated.

He shrugged and started to lean in toward her but then stopped. "If they find out you came to me for this, they will kill me too, I think. It is a risk, no?"

Kilgore sighed and pinged another thousand credits to the man's implant. His expression of doubt abruptly disappeared, and he gave her a small smile. "Very well, señorita, we get started now. Let me know if you want something to bite down on."

Then he leaned in and began using the needle to insert the pigment just under the skin of Heather's stomach. The full design, covering her stomach completely, would take most of the day to complete.

FORTY-EIGHT
COMING CLEAN
HEATHER KILGORE

Two Days Before the Rally

"OK, Zak, it's time to tell me why you're really here because there is absolutely no way the Order *or* ProSec would send an *analyst* on this mission. Time to come clean."

Next to her in the cockpit of the *Urso Dançante,* Zak Brighton fidgeted for a moment, refusing to meet her gaze. Then, slowly, he opened his mouth and started talking.

"I lied to you before, Agent Kilgore. The orders I gave you weren't from the King's Cross; in fact, they don't know I'm in Koratan space."

She nodded. Before they'd even left Novo Recife, her implant had finished its forensic analysis of the so-called orders Zak had given her about taking him along as 'support'. They were a terrific forgery and actually used a real authentication code from the King—she didn't even want to think how ProSec had gotten their hands on that. But there were telltale signs buried deep in the metadata that gave them away. She'd held off on confronting him until now, given that they'd been on the run and then surrounded by the crew of the *Urso*.

Zak didn't seem all that surprised that the revelation wasn't new to her, and he continued. "Truth is, not even ProSec wanted me to come out here, but I convinced the director we had to do something!"

He stopped, turning away from her to stare down at his hands folded in his lap.

"Do something about what?" she prompted, almost gently, after several moments of silence.

When he looked back at her, she saw fear in his eyes. Then her implant pinged as he sent something over to it. She opened the file and started to read, and abruptly, her jaw dropped open, and her eyes went wide.

"Is this what I think it is?" she asked, almost choking on the words.

Zak nodded.

"But why?" she gasped.

"We don't know," he answered simply. "What we do know is what's in that message..."

She shook her head. The word 'message' made what he'd pinged over to her sound almost pedestrian. As if anyone could think a secret communication between the Koratan president, Francisco Ignacio Juarez, and King Charles' cousin, the Duke of Serravo, was *pedestrian*! It was treason, plain and simple.

"But why would Ignacio Juarez want the King to order his own wife and daughter killed?"

Brighton shrugged. "We don't know," he repeated. "Sure, we can speculate, and we've done a lot of that. This message is dated a month before the failed Hudson invasion. Which means that Serravo knew the Koratan fleet was coming; that alone is treason on his part since he didn't warn anyone. But why he's conspiring with the Koratan president to kill the man's wife and daughter...well, we think maybe it was aimed at making sure that the war kept going or got worse.

You know, just in case the invasion at Hudson wasn't enough to enrage people on both sides. And when the invasion failed…well, maybe they were trying to do it anyway to restart the shooting war that way or to keep Ignacio Juarez in power with a sympathy vote.

"But like I said, that's all speculation, so…" he trailed off and shrugged helplessly again.

"But why would the King go along with something so…so…insane?" Heather asked in dismay and disbelief, losing any of her normal professional detachment at the horrible revelations he was dumping on her.

Zak frowned and looked back down at his hands. "Heather," he said softly; it was the first time he'd used her first name, "how often have you actually met King Charles?"

The question surprised her, and she had to think for a second. "A dozen times, usually to receive an award for service and once to get my orders directly from him for a particularly…sensitive mission." She shuddered; that had been the night her monarch had commanded her to kill his other cousin, the Duke of Kipling, along with the man's ten-year-old son.

"Have you seen him lately, in the last six months?"

"No," she responded honestly. "But that's not so unusual. He rarely meets directly with anyone in the King's Cross except the head of the Order."

Zak nodded knowingly. "What if I told you that the director of ProSec was approached six months ago by several members of the King's inner council? That they expressed concern about the King's…erratic behavior."

She looked back at him sharply. "What?"

"This isn't common knowledge, but nine months ago, Prince Gerald was diagnosed with a rare and untreatable form of cancer—it's terminal; by now, he has maybe four more months to live."

Heather's mouth dropped open in surprise for a second time in the conversation. "How does no one know about that? The heir is going to die, and no one knows?"

"The King kept it silent. He only told his inner circle, and some of them told my director, but only because they thought the news…broke King Charles. At first, he just seemed to be in mourning, even angry. But then, after a couple of months, he started acting erratically, issuing edicts that made no sense and listening more and more to some of the radicals among his advisers. Radicals like Serravo who advocated a firmer stance toward Koratas and even the Leeward Republic. It's why he went so far as to finally pull the trigger on obtaining those illegal ship parts from NSX Arms in the Inner Rim, the ones we lost at Yolandra. Because he was planning to use them against Koratas."

Heather stood without warning. Brighton startled at her move and was too stunned to say anything more as she stalked out of the cockpit, feeling the sudden urge to be alone.

She made her way to the former and unlamented captain's quarters, entering and locking the hatch behind her. It was a risk leaving the ship without a human pilot while still in the inner system near Nueva Guadalajara, where they'd dropped off the children they'd rescued from the *Urso's* crew. But it was a straight shot from the planet to the outer system and its jump point to Koratas. Besides, she couldn't stay in the same room as Zak right now; she had to *think*!

Unfortunately, after two full hours of reading and rereading the message between President Ignacio Juarez and the Promethean Duke of Serravo, she still couldn't force herself to believe that what Zak was telling her was true. Her mind kept going to all the missions she'd done over the last nine months. Had all of them been at the orders of an unbalanced and insane ruler? Or had the King's madness actually started years earlier? Had he even been in his right mind when he'd ordered her to kill the Duke of Kipling and his young son?

Was *everything* about her life a lie? All this time, all these killings, she'd convinced herself she was doing what was best for Prometheus because the King *was* Prometheus, and she had to believe he had legitimate reasons for all his orders. But if he wasn't sane...

She almost ignored the timid knock on the hatch, but when Zak knocked a third time, she got up and opened it, turning her back immediately after and returning to take a seat on the cabin's small bunk.

For a few moments, Zak stood in the hatchway, saying nothing. Then he walked in, pulled the chair out from the room's tiny desk, and turned it to face Heather. He sat down, leaning forward, and steepled his hands in front of him while he studied a random spot on the deck between them.

It was Heather who broke the silence. "How sure are you? About all of this?"

He sighed audibly and sat back, regarding her. "As sure as we can be. Half the King's advisory council have verified his questionable behavior. But we haven't been able to dig into it much further than that for obvious reasons. If it gets out, it would cause mass panic. There are only four of us in all of ProSec who even know about this, including me and the director. I'm one of his top analysts, but I'm no field agent. Still, when we decided we needed to send *someone*, I was the only one of the four who could leave Prometheus for an extended period without raising any questions. And we certainly weren't going to risk telling anyone else."

"So what, you were going to try and stop me?"

He shrugged. "Honestly, I don't know. I figured it was a losing proposition, but we had to try. We all saw that the only reasonable outcome of killing Nanette Fournier and her daughter was an all-out war. And we couldn't let *that* happen. I was told to stop you by any means possible."

She raised an eyebrow at him and huffed despite the somber topic. "No offense, but the idea of you being able to stop me is even more insane than you claim King Charles is."

He nodded. "I know. But like I said, we had to try *something*. The failed invasion gave Serravo the perfect lever to convince the King to order the deaths of the first lady and first daughter, and none of the cooler heads on the council could sway him otherwise."

"You know what this means?" she asked, her voice cold. "It means the Koratans know we're coming, and now the ones who almost caught us on Novo Recife make a whole lot more sense. Maybe they don't even want us to kill the first family; maybe what they really want is to *catch* us trying to do it so they can use it as a pretext for war. It would have almost the same effect as actually killing them, don't you think?"

"It had crossed my mind," he admitted. "And it's why I couldn't let you leave me behind on Santa Maria IV or on the starliner. I knew I'd have to gain your trust before you'd listen to me on this, even with the evidence."

They sat there in silence for several minutes, each lost in their own thoughts. This time, Zak spoke first. "So, assuming you *do* trust me on this, we are going to turn around now, right? Head back to Promethean space?"

She looked up at him and frowned. "No."

"No?" His voice took on a desperate edge. "What do you mean, no? After everything I told you, you still want to go through with it?" He stood up, knocking the chair over and standing facing her with fists clenched at his side, his jaw closed so tightly that veins stood out on his temples.

"Let me ask you something, Zak," she said calmly, almost softly. "If they really want to start a war, what do you think they'll do when I don't show up to start it for them?"

For a moment, she wasn't sure he'd even heard her. Then, all at once, his jaw unclenched, his hands relaxed, and his shoulders slumped in dejected defeat. "You think they'll do it themselves?"

She nodded. "It's what I would do. They'll have a contingency plan."

"So what? How does you going there change anything?"

It was her turn to stand up and face him, and she looked him directly in the eyes as she did so. "It might not. But if we can *stop* them, then we can avert war. But even if we do that, it probably won't be enough. Ignacio Juarez and Serravo will simply find another way."

"So, what are we going to do?" he asked, and she keyed to the fact that he said 'we' instead of 'you'. It gave her an unexpected warm feeling, even in the face of her entire paradigm being shattered to nothing, maybe *especially* in the face of that. Right now, Zak Brighton was the only true thing in her life; everything else was a lie. It didn't mean she liked him, and he was still a bumbling fool, but he was trying to do the right thing, like she should be.

For the first time in the hours since Zak's startling revelations began, Heather smiled, showing her teeth. "We need to save Nanette Fournier and her daughter…and we're going to *kill* President Ignacio Juarez. It's a risk; he's not as popular as his wife and daughter, but killing him could still launch a war. But leaving him alive means that, eventually, he'll try again anyway. Whatever he and Serravo are planning, we're going to put an end to it."

FORTY-NINE
AN OPEN QUESTION
LOLA, PRESENT DAY

The surveillance van was still where Uvalde had left it when she'd taken her doomed trip to the top of building eight. Lola roughly grabbed the first tech she came across and practically threw him into the van before his superiors could argue, not that they would have even attempted to argue with a member of the Guard.

"What am I looking for?" he asked for the second time. Apparently, he wasn't the brightest of Koratas' available security technicians.

"Get me all footage, even at an angle, of the top of building eight for five minutes before and after that shot. Now!" The way she said it ensured he didn't ask a third time, though he kept looking up at her and her white hair and gray eyes. Still, he huddled in front of his screen and started cycling through available imagery.

"Sparrow, this is Raven," the other Guard agent's voice came through Lola's implant. "No luck finding Wolf, but we did find the rifle he used ditched in a dumpster two blocks away."

She nodded to herself. It was the first lead they'd had in

nearly 30 minutes since Uvalde had called from the roof with her last dying breath.

"And?"

"Pretty standard. X-Systems 3000 rail gun. But something is funny about it."

"What?" she demanded, her patience running so thin she asked the question out loud, causing the tech to jump next to her. Lola ignored him.

"Didn't you say you saw the flash of Wolf's rifle scope from the rooftop right before the shot?"

"Yes, why?"

Raven paused before answering, and Lola was about to demand another reply when the man spoke. "The scope he used was cross-polarized with a digital shield matrix and a sunshade. No way it would have reflected the light, not unless the sun was directly behind you when you saw it."

Lola immediately understood the significance. There was no way the flashes she and Sparrow had seen—the ones that had warned them—had come from that rifle. Something else had caused them, but what?

Just then, the tech gave a little cry of triumph but then sank back down in his chair when she turned her gaze to him. "Someone commanded all our surveillance drones to stay away from building eight," he told her. "Not sure who or why—the logs were wiped—but one of them still caught footage of the rooftop on its long-range camera. It's grainy, but I can see a figure up there."

"Play it," she demanded, pinging to Raven to stand by and turning her full attention to one of the van's viewscreens. On it, she saw what was clearly video taken from very far away of the rooftop of building eight. At first, it was just that—an empty rooftop. Then, a figure detached itself from the doorway that led back down into the building's stairwell.

Even at the distance, by the size and gait of the figure, she knew it was Wolf.

She and the tech watched as the man moved in a swift crouch the last five meters to the building's balustrade, where he propped up the rifle. He sighted along it for about 30 seconds, and she could guess that he was taking final wind speed and elevation readings and feeding them into the rifle scope's AI to calculate the shot. Then, the rifle bucked in his arms—it was the only indication it had fired; railguns had no muzzle flash, and the video lacked audio—and he almost immediately started moving to leave the rooftop edge and make his way back to the stairwell exit.

"Uh, do you want me to pause?" the tech asked uncomfortably. He'd probably heard enough to know what happened next.

She didn't respond, and he let the vid keep playing. On it, a much smaller figure than Wolf came running out onto the rooftop, and the big assassin lifted his rifle and shot Hayley Uvalde in the chest, sending her tumbling down onto the hard asphalt surface of the roof.

"Pause video," she finally commanded the tech, ignoring the whimpering of Katarina and Trina as they relived Uvalde's death through Lola's eyes. Victoria had huddled into her usual corner, pretending to sleep, and Sparrow…

…Lola couldn't even feel Sparrow in her head. It was as if the other woman, the supposed core personality who governed all of them, had ceased to exist altogether. Lola couldn't say she would miss her. With Sparrow out of the way, she would have full control. The others were too weak—too timid—to take over unless Lola let them.

"Reverse back to right before the shot," she ordered the tech, and he hastened to comply. Then, she had him run it frame by frame.

"There!" she cried out, jabbing a finger at the screen so hard she almost broke it. "Right there! You see it?"

The tech stammered but then looked closer, squinting at the screen. "I don't get it. It's probably just a lens flare or a bad pixel in the image."

Lola shook her head emphatically. It wasn't. It was the flash—the first one—she and Sparrow had seen. And it hadn't come from the rifle scope. She studied the single point of momentary light more closely. Not only had it not come from the rifle scope, but it hadn't even come from the rooftop. Instead, the flash was suspended in the air 20 meters above the rooftop and behind the building, where it had a direct line of sight over Wolf's shoulder to the stage.

"I thought you said there were no drones in the vicinity when he took the shot," she said to the tech, almost accusatorially.

He squirmed in his seat. "There weren't. If that's a drone, it's not one of ours. But how did it get past our scans of the area? It shouldn't even have been there."

She ignored his last few words and turned away. "Fox," she called over her implant. "Did the crime scene techs finish processing the van?"

"They did," the woman replied almost instantly. "Found evidence of two occupants, one with red hair dyed black, almost certainly the woman. Based on the thermal signatures left on the seats, the man was driving, and she was in the back taking the shot."

"Did they find anything else?" she demanded. "Anything that didn't fit?"

The connection was silent for a second, and she could almost hear Fox asking the techs around her the same question. Then, the other agent was back. "Now that you mention it, they found an AI controller. They're not sure what it's for, but it looks like the type that could be used for—"

"A drone," Lola interrupted.

"Sí, how did you know?"

She didn't answer, cutting the connection as brusquely as Wolf had often done to Sparrow. It made no sense. Why would the King's Cross agents use a drone to purposefully warn her of Wolf's impending shot? Were they trying to prevent him from taking it?

Maybe they aren't King's Cross? Maybe one of ours? Katarina suggested timidly, but Lola ignored her. Maybe the other woman was right, but that didn't change the fact that Lola was going to kill Wolf and whoever had killed the president and sent that drone. It was the only way this would end.

She opened a comm channel to Fox and Raven. "Listen, the King's Cross was working with Wolf," she lied, drawing a startled gasp from Katarina and a choking gurgle from Trina. "They are all to be considered primary targets. Find them, and then call me immediately to dispatch them."

Both agents acknowledged Lola's orders and signed off to go get started.

Why would the King's Cross save Estrella Ignacio? Trina whispered.

And why did you lie about it? Katarina said, her voice trembling.

Lola ignored them both. They simply didn't understand. It just didn't matter who or why had done what today. All of them were going to die by her hand. It was the way she would prove herself the dominant personality, the best of them, not just of those inside Sparrow's head, but of the entire Confederate Guard.

She left the van and the terrified tech behind and stalked out into the waning daylight, another smile on her lips.

FIFTY
BREAKING WALLS
HEATHER KILGORE

They'd left the cover of the abandoned apartment as soon as the sun started going down. They didn't have time to wait until full darkness, and in Heather's experience, twilight was almost as good for moving stealthily, especially in an urban environment fraught with shadows from surrounding buildings.

Regardless, they got out only minutes before a Koratan police squad entered the building they'd been hiding in and started a floor-to-floor search. She could only hope they didn't have imagery of them yet, or if they did, the old man they'd helped with his groceries wouldn't remember their faces well enough to ID them. Just in case, she tore her shirt, exposing her stomach and the large tattoo there—the one she'd had inked on her two weeks ago on Santa Maria IV. It might draw glances from the citizens they passed, terrified ones at that, but it was also the best cover she had right now, just as she'd intended it to be.

Now, they were two blocks away, but not directly away from the park; rather, they moved clockwise around it, maintaining the same general distance. The cordon of roadblocks and police presence would be tight *everywhere*, but most humans couldn't maintain a constant state of vigilance and readiness for very long. Heather hoped that the police manning the various roadblocks and checkpoints would be starting to think that maybe they'd already slipped through the inner perimeter or that they might try and do so close to where they'd disappeared.

She was grasping at straws, and she knew it. Every police officer, federal investigator, security officer, and poodle in the area would be on an insanely heightened level of vigilance and even jumpiness after the violent death of their president. There was virtually no chance any of them would be letting down their guard any time soon.

So, Heather and Zak were faced with the age-old dilemma of the prey in any hunt: stay still and hope the predator didn't find you, or keep moving and hope you could keep out of its grasp.

At least, in this case, the prey could also fight back.

They approached a roadblock four blocks away from the building they'd hid in and stopped in the shadows half a block away. Heather studied the area while Zak kept an eye on their rear in case someone had seen them slipping through the shadows and followed them. So far, they'd been lucky; not even the ever-present drones overhead had seemed to take an undue interest in them. It helped that there were still a fair amount of other people out on the street, mostly gathering in small groups and talking in animated fashion about both the events of a few blocks away and the shutdown of their section of the city. It allowed Heather and Zak's thermal images to blend in with the regular citizens here and there.

"Anything?" Zak whispered harshly. They were both under tremendous stress, but he was showing it more than Heather. She ignored his tone and pointed to a building across the street for him to see.

"That building connects to the one next to it via a shared basement, assuming we can believe the city records. That will get us right up to the roadblock unseen. Then we can get to the roof and from there to the roof of the adjoining building on the other side of the roadblock."

He followed her gaze, and she could almost feel him stiffen behind her. "You want to go from *that* rooftop to *that* one? They're not even the same height? And they've gotta be, what, ten meters apart?"

"More like six," she replied evenly. "And don't they teach you to hit the ground rolling in ProSec?"

"They also taught us how to cauterize our own gut wound with a hot knife, but that doesn't mean I want to try it any time soon," he quipped, and she was heartened to see he still had his sense of humor. Maybe he wasn't dealing as poorly with the stress as she worried.

"Well, no time like the present to put your training to use," she said. "I'll cross the street first; they'll be looking for a man and a woman together. You backtrack a half block, cross down there, and then meet me in the lobby of that first building. Got it?"

It took five tense minutes before he finally met her in the indicated building's lobby. As far as she could tell, and she had been watching, the police hadn't given either of them too long of a glance. It helped that they'd been wearing reversible jackets when they'd fled the van and now had them inside out. The twilight also helped.

She led him wordlessly down a stairwell into the building's basement. It was a drab and dusty space, poorly lit and filled with boxes that looked like they could almost predate the war with Prometheus. Together, they followed the map in Heather's implant, using the plans on file with the city planning office she'd hacked into as soon as they'd arrived on planet. It took them down a long corridor lined with storage and machine rooms until they came to a door that was supposed to lead into a shared space between the two buildings.

Heather opened it and, after a brief sweep of her eyes for threats, stepped through to find…

…a dead end.

Where the basement of the next building should have been was a blank wall, clearly erected to divide and separate the basements of the two buildings without updating the city planning office. The wall looked like it had been there a long time.

Heather swore aloud and quickly searched the small room from corner to corner, finding no other doors, so she turned and started walking back the way they'd come.

"Wait," Brighton admonished her. She turned to see him step up to the wall and start knocking on it.

"What are you doing?" she asked.

"Old buildings like this, they make changes all the time without filing them, but the owners are aways worried that the city might send an inspector and flag them for remodeling without a permit. So they tend to…got it!" He reached back a hand and punched hard into the wall, breaking cleanly through it.

Heather gaped.

"As I was saying," Zak said as he started to use the edges of the hole to pull apart the drywall around it. They tend to make the changes as cheaply as they can so they can tear them down if a building inspector demands it. So they're not built to be sturdy or really to last. In this case, the wall is a simple metal frame with cheap drywall; it doesn't even have any insulation."

He beckoned her over and showed her his progress: a basketball-sized hole in their side of the wall that went through to a slightly smaller hole in the opposite drywall.

Through it, they could see a dark room, and Heather's implant enhanced her lowlight vision until she could see they were looking into a space nearly identical to the one they were in now.

"How do you know all this?" she asked him as she joined his effort to pull and push away more of the drywall on both sides.

"Dad was in construction, sort of the family business. Wasn't too happy when his only son went off to become a spy. How about you? Your parents proud you joined the Order?"

The hole had become just big enough for Heather to slip through between the metal frames to either side, and she did so both to start breaking the drywall from the other side and to avoid answering Zak's question. She found herself in an identical room in the other building's basement, empty save for a few stacked chairs and a single door on the far side.

Within another minute, the hole was big enough for Zak to push his way through. Mission accomplished: they were in the next building, the one right next to the roadblock but still on the wrong side of it.

Heather looked at Zak and grinned. "Ready to jump off a roof?"

FIFTY-ONE
EXTENDING THE PERIMETER
LOLA

"The locals want to extend the perimeter and move all the roadblocks back a couple of blocks," Fox told Lola as she jogged through the nearly empty streets looking for her quarry. It was almost pointless for her to be out here looking; even with the narrow five-block radius they'd set up around the park, the area inside the perimeter was nearly four square kilometers. Not to mention that almost a hundred thousand people lived in that perimeter, giving the missing King's Cross agents ample places to hide.

But Lola knew she could direct the efforts just as well from the streets using her implant as she could from the surveillance van or command post at the park. In fact, maybe even better, because none of the locals could argue her orders to her face. Plus, being out here would keep her closer to the location where the enemy was likely to be found so that she could be the one to kill them.

"Tell them to keep the current perimeter but set up a secondary four more blocks out," she told the other agent.

"They say they'll need to call in every precinct across the city to have that kind of manpower," Fox replied.

"Tell them that every single one of them will be fired if they let the assassins through!" she snapped back, and Fox acknowledged her order and closed the connection. She'd not even had time to stop and wonder why Fox and Raven, both senior to Sparrow in tenure with the Guard, had so easily fallen in line with taking Lola's orders. Maybe it was because she'd taken charge when Wolf's absence had left a sudden vacuum of leadership. Or maybe they were hoping that mission failure would blow back on Sparrow rather than them.

Either way, it didn't matter. There would be plenty of blame to go around if they failed to catch the president's killers…and Wolf. But Lola didn't plan on failing.

She jogged around a corner and saw one of the police-manned roadblocks just a block away. She moved toward it, pinging Sparrow's credentials ahead so that they wouldn't shoot at her—leave it to the local cops to probably be ready to fire at anything that moved at this point—and even from a distance, she could see the moment they read her pinged ID. They all stiffened and looked nervous. Usually, members of the Guard used cover identities, even with other intelligence or law enforcement agencies. But not today. Not when their nation's head of state had been killed just blocks away.

Lola loped up to the officer who was clearly in charge. "Report!" she barked, and the man immediately began stammering his way through a clumsy summary that basically amounted to nothing. As he talked, she scanned the surrounding buildings.

"Do you have anyone in those two buildings?" she interrupted the police lieutenant's monologue, pointing to the closest buildings on either side of the street.

He looked momentarily confused, then nodded slowly. "Sure, uh, two officers each. In case they try and slip by us that way, though not sure how that would work. But it's protocol." He said the last almost proudly as if he wanted a cookie or a medal for following the rules.

"Two won't be enough," she said, still studying the buildings. "Send another squad each into both buildings."

"But protocol says to only send two—"

His argument cut off in a startled gasp when she reached up and grabbed him by the collar, jerking his face down to meet hers. "Send. Another. Squad. Each."

This time, the man didn't even try to argue, turning and indicating to eight of his police officers to move in groups of four into each of the indicated buildings. Shaking her head as she watched, Lola sent a ping to the makeshift command post in the park, ordering the locals there by the authority of the Guard to do the same thing at the other checkpoints.

FIFTY-TWO
US VS. THEM
HEATHER KILGORE

The elevator bank in the building's lobby was in full view of the street and the police at the roadblock outside, so Heather took Zak up the stairs to the second floor to catch the lift there. It was a testament to the stress they were both under that they didn't notice the approaching cop until she was right on top of them.

Luckily, she didn't notice them either until they rounded the staircase landing and practically bumped into her. And instead of screaming in fright, which might have actually saved her, the police officer did the brave but stupid thing.

She went for her gun.

Heather's knife was already in her hand from where she'd had it hidden in her long shirt sleeve. As the cop cleared the gun from her holster, the knife pierced the side of her neck. Both of the woman's hands flew to her throat, the gun clattering away down the stairs. It was the last move she would ever make, and less than two seconds later, she lay dead on the stairwell landing.

"That was..." Brighton said, and she could see him

turning white, marveling again how squeamish he was for a ProSec agent.

"Necessary," she finished before he could say whatever was on his mind. "It was her or us."

"But she was a cop! Not an enemy, a cop!" he said more than a little too loudly, and she winced as his voice echoed up and down the stairway.

"Listen," she hissed, grabbing him hard by the arm and practically yanking him up the remaining stairs with her. "If we're going to survive this, you have to get one thing straight. There are no good guys and bad guys here right now. Just us and the people trying to kill us. Maybe that cop was ready for sainthood, but she still would have put a bullet into us, or arrested us, or screamed for help, all of which is the same thing. If we're captured, it will give whoever is backing Ignacio Juarez and the Duke of Serravo exactly what they need to start this war. The best thing we can do is keep moving and avoid trouble so we don't have to kill anyone else. But if we can't, then we strike first, and we strike hard."

She left him to consider that in silence as they reached the second floor and called the lift. It was a risk to take it—if someone found the dead cop before they reached the top of the building, they could command the elevator's AI to stop the car between floors and effectively trap them inside. But taking the stairs all the way to the 50th floor of the high-rise apartment building would have taken them far too long.

When they arrived on the top floor, they stepped out into a blessedly empty but very ornate hallway. Just as Heather had hoped, they quickly found the stairs up to the roof, though the door had a physical lock and was too heavily reinforced to kick in, so Heather had to stop and take the time to pick it. It was time they probably didn't have.

FIFTY-THREE
QUARRY FOUND
LOLA

Lola didn't need to see the look on the police lieutenant's face to know that one of his squads had found the dead body of a fellow officer in the building to their right. She was already tapped into his comm feed, and she didn't wait for him to relay the news before she started sprinting toward the building and calling out orders to his entire contingent of officers.

She found the body on the landing to the second floor, a large pool of blood underneath it from a severed carotid artery.

Lola started barking more orders. She sent two squads up, one in each lift, to start at the top floors and begin searching back toward street level, while two more squads would do the same from the bottom up. She couldn't afford to pull any more than that, or she would leave the roadblock outside unguarded, which might be exactly what the King's Cross agents were hoping she'd do. But she started calling in support from elsewhere in the city and almost screamed in frustration at how long it would take them to get there.

FIFTY-FOUR
LEAP OF FAITH
HEATHER KILGORE

"Ready for this?"

Next to Heather, Zak Brighton swallowed whatever response he might have made and swayed back from the rooftop. It was a *long* way down, and there was no guarantee they could bridge the gap to the next building, which was about six meters away horizontally.

"That's a really long way down, and we don't have anti-grav," he finally choked out, but she didn't know if he was referring to the 50-story drop if they missed the other building or the fact that the other building's rooftop was almost two stories below the one they stood on now. She agreed with him on both counts.

"Just think, if you miss, you'll be dead almost before you realize you're going to die," she said and then backed up and started sprinting toward the edge of the building.

"That's not as comforting as you think it..." she heard him say as she ran past, but his words were lost in the rush of wind as she hit the rooftop's edge, stepped up onto the short balustrade, and leapt out into the night sky.

For a moment, as she reached the zenith of her jump, there was an almost preternatural stillness around her, like she was floating in zero-g vacuum. But just as suddenly, the entire world seemed to fly upward, and she felt her stomach fighting its way up her throat as she plummeted toward the distant rooftop below.

She hit hard but allowed her knees to crumple under her and her body to roll several times across the soft dirt of what was, thankfully, the rooftop garden she had aimed for. Even so, she felt her knees, elbows, and hips hit the dirt hard enough during her mad tumble that she knew there would be some nasty bruises later.

Finally stopping her roll and pulling herself to her feet, she looked back up at the higher building she'd jumped from. At first, she saw nothing, and she wondered if Zak had chickened out and decided just to turn himself into the Koratans or try his luck hiding somewhere in the building. Then, his form came hurtling off the rooftop's edge, and she watched as he flailed his arms and legs and let loose a high-pitched scream that—probably—couldn't be heard all the way below at street level.

He hit harder than her but still managed to roll through the dirt. But when he stopped, and she hastened over to help him to his feet, he grunted in pain as he put weight on his right ankle. Heather watched in horror as it collapsed beneath him.

"Broken?" she asked, trying to keep her voice calm and clinical despite the panic she now felt welling up inside her.

Thankfully, he shook his head. "Probably sprained. I just need a second."

Despite the fact that they didn't have a second to spare, she let him catch his breath and gingerly test putting gradual weight onto the ankle. Though he winced as he did so, he was able to walk a few steps, albeit with a pronounced limp.

"Let's go," he said through gritted teeth, and she led the way toward the rooftop exit. They ditched their dirt-covered jackets as they went; they would only draw more attention.

FIFTY-FIVE
ORDERS AND THREATS

LOLA

"Where are my drones?" Lola demanded into her implant comm back to the police commissioner at the command post.

"They were needed elsewhere in the city. It's a big place, and..." the pompous man on the other end of the line started to explain, his tone like that of an adult speaking to an unruly child.

She cut him off by having her implant send a squelching noise that was calculated to pierce the inside of his head like an ice pick. He stopped off whatever he was going to say next, and she spoke before he could regain his composure.

"If there aren't two drones over my position in the next 60 seconds, I will hunt you down and kill you without a second's thought. Understand imbecille?"

For an instant, she thought he might still argue, but despite her pronouncement being patently illegal, there were enough rumors about the Guard circulating that he'd probably believe both that she could and that she would. And Lola was actually willing to do it. He'd made her so upset she'd let split some of her Italian accent and even called the man an imbecile in Italian. But if the commissioner caught either, he didn't bring it up. Sounding wounded and scared, he acknowledged her command, and her implant's map showed her two blue dots flying rapidly toward her from a few blocks away.

As she looked up in the night sky to try and spot their running lights, something about the roof of the building where they'd found the dead police officer stopped her. She studied it for a moment, then swore in her native tongue.

"All units converge on me. They're in the next building over!" she yelled out loud, letting her implant relay it to those who were not within the sound of her voice.

FIFTY-SIX
SLOWING DOWN

HEATHER KILGORE

In the lift ride down from the rooftop, Heather used the brief respite to fashion a crude wrap for Brighton's ankle with strips she'd torn from her discarded jacket. He experimentally put more weight on the limb and then nodded to her encouragingly, though she could see the great globs of sweat breaking out on his forehead as he tried not to let the pain show.

She took a deep breath and let it out as the elevator door opened on the third floor, and they disembarked so she could help him down the stairs to street level.

Once there—it took *way* too long for Zak to go down the two flights—she led him down what looked like a service corridor to an emergency exit that had all sorts of warning labels. She overrode the door's basic AI controller so that when she pushed it open, no alarm sounded. They found themselves in an alley with exits on both sides. Rolling the dice mentally, Heather pulled Zak to the right and toward the street beyond.

FIFTY-SEVEN
QUARRY LOST
LOLA

Lola wanted to scream. Either they'd missed the King's Cross fugitives by seconds, or she'd made the wrong call in pulling the police from the first building to the second on her hunch that they'd crossed the rooftops. Either way, her quarry had eluded her, and the drones now overhead hadn't picked them up in time either.

Briefly, she considered her next move. It never even occurred to her to call Nest or any of the other Guard leadership on planet. She knew, even if she doubted Sparrow would ever admit it, that there was no way Wolf had been acting alone. Chances were, someone in the upper echelons of the Guard was in on his plan to kill the president's daughter. Something far bigger than any of them realized was in play here.

Plus, she simply didn't want their help. Sparrow might trust Nest, but Lola never had, and she didn't want anyone swooping in and taking these kills away from her. Besides, she imagined they were busy dealing with the fallout of the president's death and probably securing the surviving members of the first family.

Letting out a long breath, Lola made a decision. It would have horrified Sparrow—junior agents like her simply didn't do things like this—but Sparrow was nowhere to be found, despite Katarina, Trina, and even Victoria desperately searching for her in the recesses of their shared mind.

"All units," Lola said somberly, "this is the Confederate Guard, authorization blockchain attached to this message. I am hereby ordering a city-wide curfew, effective immediately. Any citizens not indoors within the next twenty minutes are to be detained or shot on sight. Deadly force is authorized for any who resist."

FIFTY-EIGHT
CURFEW

HEATHER KILGORE

Heather grunted in frustration as she looked around the corner at the street beyond.

"What is it?" Zak asked behind her. She could hear the strain in his voice, though he'd gamely limped along next to her for the last four blocks since they'd left the building they'd jumped onto. And despite his slow pace, they'd gotten past what was clearly a new outer perimeter for their searchers, and they'd watched as the local police had setup a roadblock about a block behind them.

"Tune your implant to the civil broadcast station," she told him. "Receive mode only."

A second later, she heard him use some fairly choice words that were very out of character with his straitlaced personality. "A curfew in a city of 50 million people? Isn't that a bit extreme?"

She looked back at him and shrugged. "Imagine if the Guard came to Prometheus and killed King Charles."

He frowned but nodded back. "You're right. The queen would probably order the entire system to be locked down until they found them. We're pretty screwed, aren't we?"

She shook her head, though it was hard to keep up a brave face. They were dirty and tired, and now they would be alone on the streets, easy pickings for the drones overhead. She could already see that most citizens were heading inside, and soon, the streets would be empty.

"Leave me here," Zak said, drawing a surprised glance from her.

"What?"

"Leave me here. I'm only going to slow you down. Without me, you can move faster and get away. I'll find someplace to hunker down, and hopefully, they'll miss me in the sweeps."

He said the last part like he didn't believe it, nor did she.

"We don't leave agents behind," she said curtly and turned back to study the street.

He didn't reply, so she grabbed his arm and pulled him behind her and onto the broad avenue. She stayed close to the buildings on each side and used the few people still out on the sidewalks to hopefully mask their movements from above.

He was right. They really had no hope of getting out of this, and she *should* leave him behind. He wasn't a member of the Order, only ProSec, so she technically did not have the same obligations to him as she would have had to a fellow King's Cross agent. Protocol demanded that she not allow herself to be captured along with the secrets in her head, even if it meant abandoning him, though she'd have to kill him to keep the Koratans from interrogating him.

Of course, Heather scoffed internally, she wasn't all that good at following protocol when it came to leaving a man behind. First the farm boy on Hudson; now, the ProSec agent on Koratas. One of these days, her stubbornness was going to get her killed.

Probably today.

FIFTY-NINE
PICKING UP THE TRAIL
LOLA

"Drone 17 has movement in the northeast sector," Fox reported calmly into Lola's head.

"Where exactly?" she asked eagerly.

"Three and a half blocks due west of your position, heading away from you," the other agent answered.

Motioning to the squad of local cops with her, Lola started running in the indicated direction, sensing that the pursuit would finally be over soon. She'd kill the King's Cross agents, and then she'd go hunting Wolf.

SIXTY
TAKING SHELTER

HEATHER KILGORE

A car would be great right now; it would also be useless. Even if the police hadn't shut down the roads when they first started looking for Kilgore and Brighton, the curfew meant that any car still out would be subject to being immediately stopped and searched.

No, their only hope was to run or hide. In the end, predictably, Zak's ankle made the decision for them.

They were jogging the best they could down a nearly deserted street when Heather heard the man gasp in pain behind her and fall to his knees. She turned.

"You OK?" It was a stupid question. Zak was drenched in sweat, and his jaw was clenched so tight that it was making all the veins in his head stand out even more than when he'd faced her down on the *Urso*.

"I'll…be…fine," he gasped, but she wasn't buying it.

She studied the buildings around them. All were brightly lit, the citizens inside hunkered down for the curfew. She saw a few dark windows that might have denoted an empty apartment or office but might also simply be darkened bedrooms of otherwise occupied homes.

Then, she saw a figure round the corner a block ahead of them, jogging briskly their way, and she stiffened. The way the person moved, they were an operator. No question about it.

Hastily, and hopefully before the distant figure could see them in the dark shadows, she helped Zak hobble back the way they came to an alley mouth they'd passed, where they ducked inside.

SIXTY-ONE
CLOSING IN

LOLA

"You're two minutes out," Fox reported in Lola's head. "Drone shows they've gone to ground in an alley. By the way one of them is moving—looks like the man—he's injured."

"Any energy signatures?" Lola asked as she kept running. The cops with her slowly fell behind when they couldn't keep up with her relentless pace.

"Nothing the drones can detect. So, no lasers and probably no railguns. But that doesn't rule out conventional ballistic arms. Watch yourself," came Fox's reply.

Lola didn't answer, cutting the connection as she started readying for the kill.

SIXTY-TWO
SACRIFICES

HEATHER KILGORE

The alley was a dead end, with a brick wall blocking the far end. The only doors were sealed shut using conventional locks, and there was no external access. Without a crowbar or a laser, there was no way they'd get any of them open.

Heather was about to pull Zak back out to the street when the sound of rapidly approaching running footsteps made her push him back behind a dumpster instead, motioning for him to be quiet.

It didn't matter. She watched morosely as a figure stopped right in front of the open end of the alley and started moving slowly toward their hiding spot, the moonlight glinting off a pistol in their hand.

Heather knew she'd only get one shot at this. She drew the knife from its holster in her sleeve and grasped it tightly in her right hand, waiting and counting their pursuer's steps to be sure they would get close enough to…

She was about to spring out from behind the dumpster and trust her knife against her enemy's gun, but just as she tensed her muscles to move, a large hand and the attached arm reached around from behind and pulled and then pushed her back as Zak Brighton jumped out from around her and toward the approaching killer.

What followed happened very quickly, but not too fast for Heather to take it in. Zak never stood a chance. The large man who had followed them into the alley was a trained fighter. He was also better armed. Even as Zak flew at him, the pistol barked once, and she watched in horror as Zak reacted like someone had punched him in the stomach.

Then, she was moving, using Zak's still-falling body for cover to get close enough to leap at the larger man. His gun spat again, and she felt the bullet burn along her side as it luckily only grazed her. After that, Heather was on him.

He tried to bring the gun around as her blade took him in the shoulder, her aim for his throat spoiled by his sudden movement. He grunted in pain but otherwise didn't cry out. Instead, he shot again, and she felt the explosion of the gun close by but nothing else; he had missed her a second time!

Her next move was to hit the wrist holding the gun with her forearm, and the weapon dropped from the man's grasp and clattered to the pavement. From there, the two assassins fought desperately, Guard—because that's what he surely was—versus King's Cross.

For a little while, Heather thought she might win, especially as her knife bit deeply into the man's quadricep when he let her get a little too close. But then, he hit her with one of his large fists right in the side of the head.

It was the hardest blow Heather had ever felt, and it was only by the miracle that she was already moving in the same direction as his fist that kept it from knocking her out cold. Still, it sent her sprawling to the hard pavement, and her vision swam, clearing just in time to see the man step toward her and wind up a foot to smash into her face and end the fight and her life.

Just before that foot started to swing toward her, there was another gunshot, and the man in front of her grunted. Through the tears clouding her eyes, Heather looked behind her to see Zak Brighton, blood soaking the front of his shirt, propping himself up against one of the alley walls and holding the Guard agent's pistol; he'd obviously crawled to retrieve it while she and her attacker were busy fighting.

Still, the big man in front of her did little more than grunt in pain and stagger back a step. Then he straightened and started toward Zak.

Body armor! She'd heard about the Koratans experimenting with a type of body armor that could make itself instantly rigid against a fast-moving projectile. As she watched now, the front of the big man's shirt, which looked as solid as a board, abruptly softened and fell to hang limply from his frame again. Funny that it hadn't blocked her knife thrusts; they must not have had enough kinetic energy for the fabric to react.

Either way, it meant they were dead unless Zak shot the guy in the face, and he looked to be barely able to keep the gun up even where he had it, much less raise it higher as the big assassin moved toward him.

Then, the large man turned at the sound of running feet and shouts. Moving far more quickly than a man his size had any right to, he whirled and fled the alley and whoever was approaching.

Heather was about to rush back to Zak and try to help him up so they could find cover, but he shook his head violently as she got to her feet.

"That's…the guy…saw him…on the drone. Go!" He choked out the last word with a raspy, wet sound, and she saw that his mouth was full of blood. Before she could argue or even take a step toward him, she watched in almost slow motion as he turned the gun on himself.

The blast was loud in the alley and snapped her out of her shock just long enough for her to pick up her knife—the gun had flung itself somewhere out of sight when Zak had used it—and she made her own way to the mouth of the alley and out into the street beyond. As she sprinted for all she was worth, hot tears came to her eyes, and she tried to banish the photo-perfect image her brain had taken of Zak Brighton's last instant of life.

SIXTY-THREE
DOGS
LOLA

Lola wasn't livid. She was beyond livid.

She'd arrived at the alley too late to stop the two figures that had run from it. She'd tried to pursue them on foot, but they had both lost her, taking separate directions and leaving her to hesitate just a moment too long in deciding which one to chase.

She'd ultimately chosen to go after the woman—the surviving King's Cross agent—but she'd wanted so *badly* to go after Wolf instead. Just as she'd recognized his form and gait from the long-distance camera earlier, there was no mistaking him this time, even in the darkened streets. Still, he'd gotten away, and so had the woman.

The other King's Cross agent hadn't been so lucky, and five minutes after giving up on her pursuit of the female assassin, Lola was crouching down in front of the faceless body of a well-built man probably in his early thirties.

"Anything on the drones?" she asked Raven and Fox for the fourth time since arriving back at the alley.

"Nada," Raven replied. "They lost Wolf and the woman. Sorry, boss."

It was the first time either of the other agents had called her boss out loud, but it gave her no satisfaction. Because right now, she was angry enough to murder them if they didn't follow her orders.

"Call it in," she told Raven; he was the further away of the two. "Fox, meet me at my location. We're going to end this."

Then she turned to an out-of-breath police captain, who was trying her best to direct with hand motions the search of her other nearby officers while not throwing up at the sight of the mutilated body in the alley.

"You have dogs?" she asked the woman.

The captain nodded but was still too winded to speak. She'd tried to follow Lola in her pursuit of the female King's Cross agent—she'd even stuck with her for the first block.

"Get them here, now!"

SIXTY-FOUR
ONLY A MATTER OF TIME

HEATHER KILGORE

The sound of the dogs barking in the distance at first didn't register with Kilgore. Whether it was because she was too stunned by Zak's sudden death to notice or simply because dogs barking in a city like Koratas was a near-constant sound didn't matter. By the time Heather realized what the barking meant, it was too late.

Even in the city, the dogs should have no problem finding her scent; it was all over that alley where she'd left Zak's body.

She couldn't go to ground now. The dogs would follow her to wherever she tried to hide. She couldn't even run fast enough to escape them and the drones overhead.

But she would try anyway.

SIXTY-FIVE
CONTACT
LOLA

"Contact!" Fox practically yelled in Lola's head. "Putting it on your map now. I'm close, and I'll meet you en route. Go!"

Lola shoved one of the local cops off the hovercycle he'd just parked outside the alley with the dead King's Cross agent in it. He protested, but she ignored him, throttling the bike and jetting off toward the red glowing dot superimposed on her vision by her implant.

SIXTY-SIX
BACK TO THE BEGINNING

HEATHER KILGORE

Heather stopped running and leaned back hard against the rough brick wall, heaving great gasping breaths and trying desperately to collect her thoughts. The wall was rough and sharp through her thin, sweat-soaked, torn shirt, but the coolness of the brick felt good against her skin in the warmth of the summer night.

She slowed her breathing as best she could and strained to listen. The barking of the dogs had stopped. Did that mean they had lost her scent in the city's morass? Or had their handlers quieted them so as not to alert her of their close approach?

It almost didn't matter. She'd been running for so long already that she needed a brief respite, or she was likely to make a mistake. But now, images of a different blood-spattered alley filled her thoughts; she hadn't had time to process what had happened there, was it less than half an hour before?

A sound at the open end of the alley ripped her out of her own head and back into the moment. It had been a small noise like a foot lightly scuffing the pavement, but it portended far bigger and more dangerous things.

She glanced quickly around the dumpster that shielded her from view deep in the narrow space and resisted the urge to swear out loud. She *hadn't* lost them. And as they moved down the alley toward her, assault rifles extended on their slings and scanning back and forth, she knew the end had come.

She pulled out the only weapon left to her. Guns ran out of ammunition, even modern railguns that required only a few grams of metal and could store hundreds of shots before running dry. But a knife never ran out. It was one of the many reasons she'd always preferred her blade over a gun in so many situations.

This was not one of them.

But there was nothing to be done about it. The alley was closed off by a tall fence behind her, and there was no way she could scale that in plain view of her pursuers before they riddled her with dozens of rounds. She might as well go out fighting then, even if the outcome would be the same.

Heather Kilgore took a deep breath, tightened her grip on the knife's hilt, made slick with her sweat, and stepped calmly out from behind the dumpster and toward her death.

SIXTY-SEVEN
THE KILL
LOLA

Lola and Fox moved slowly into the alleyway, assault rifles commandeered from the local cops held out in front of them. They wore face masks; no use letting their enemy see their features on the off chance that she got away. Usually, they wouldn't worry about such things, but this particular quarry had proven to be more resilient and resourceful than any other Lola had ever encountered. Fox had practically insisted on following protocol and wearing the masks.

They were near the dumpster where Lola was sure their quarry must be hiding when a tall, lithe woman with black, sweat-soaked clothes clinging to her stepped out from behind it. Lola's finger tightened on the trigger.

She stopped, curiosity momentarily outweighing her excitement at finally running down her quarry. The dark-haired woman—it was definitely a dye job—was armed only with a knife that she held close to her body. Her shirt was ripped, exposing her stomach. On it was a very recognizable tattoo. Clever. It wouldn't work; they all knew exactly who had sent her, but it was clever nonetheless. It would have almost certainly thrown the locals off the scent, but not Lola.

"Drop the knife!" she yelled, her voice hard and her Italian accent coming through clearly. If Fox, next to her, noticed the strange change in her voice, she made no indication.

The King's Cross agent said nothing and didn't move; she just stood by the dumpster and waited. The knife was still held close in by her body and up, not too far from her own neck. Lola understood; the enemy agent was going to kill herself rather than be captured. So why hadn't she already—

The woman's eyes flicked toward Fox, but the warning was too late as Lola heard the other Guard agent next to her gasp and hit the ground hard. She whirled in time to see Wolf, his gun trained squarely on Lola now, grin and wipe the knife he'd used to slit Fox's throat off on his pants. She didn't dare move her rifle to cover him; she'd never make it in time.

"Why?" she asked him; she really didn't care, but she hoped the question would buy her time.

"Orders," he said simply. "We serve the president."

The realization hit every personality in Sparrow's head, except Lola, like a gut punch. The president had ordered the murder of his own daughter?! Why?

Plans within plans, Katarina whispered. *He wanted to get reelected, and no one would dare criticize a grieving father or come out against him publicly. He was going for the sympathy vote.*

"No, that's impossible," Lola said, pitching her voice as if she were in disbelief of his words, but again, really just trying to keep him talking.

Wolf smiled. "What, thought that we were the good guys? I have news for you, little Sparrow. There are no good guys. If you learn that, maybe I can let you live."

He studied her for a moment and then shook his head. "No. You're too much of a believer. I'm afraid this is where your story ends...and hers," he motioned with his large head toward the King's Cross agent, who hadn't moved a centimeter, and kept his gun focused on Lola.

Deep inside her, Lola felt a stirring, like someone waking up. But she ignored it and made her move, leaping to the side as she swung her assault rifle toward Wolf. Still, even she knew she'd be too late, and she could almost see the moment Wolf's finger tightened on his gun's trigger. She braced herself and resolved that she would live long enough to kill him in return. She would...

The knife appeared in Wolf's throat out of nowhere, and Lola grunted as she landed on the hard asphalt on her shoulder. The knife was almost certainly enough to kill the big man, but she pulled the assault rifle's trigger anyway, stitching him with three bullets to his unarmored face.

He fell in a slump to the pavement, dead before he hit the ground, and Lola grinned in exultation. But there was no time to celebrate as she rolled over onto her back and pointed her gun toward the King's Cross agent, who, after throwing the knife at Wolf, stood with hands outstretched to each side to show she was unarmed.

Lola didn't care, and she smiled with her teeth as she started to pull the trigger. The woman had robbed her of the chance to kill Wolf, but at least she would have the honor of murdering an Agent of the King's Cross this night!

No! screamed Katarina, Trina, and Victoria together, and the three of them did the mental equivalent of tackling Lola, who snarled and fought back viciously. Even together, they weren't enough to stop her, and the momentary loosening of her trigger finger reversed as she prepared to take the shot.

"No!" another voice screamed...through Lola's mouth. Suddenly, a raging fire burned through her mind, severing her connection to the body she'd been controlling and sending the assassin tumbling through her brain away from the light.

Sparrow! She'd thought the woman gone, but she came roaring back and took control from Lola, almost as if the assassin weren't even there.

SIXTY-EIGHT
REPRIEVE

HEATHER KILGORE

Heather watched in shock as the woman on the ground screamed and threw aside the assault rifle she'd been holding. She'd been preparing herself for that weapon to send her out of this world, but then the surviving Guard agent had, for just a second, almost looked like she was fighting herself, thrashing on the ground as one hand ripped the rifle out of the other and sent it careening toward the alley wall.

She should have taken that moment to run, but she was rooted in place by her surprise. Then, the woman in front of her stood up and stared her down, heaving great breaths as if she'd just truly been in a fight for her life.

SIXTY-NINE
REASONS
SPARROW

Sparrow got up as Lola retreated sullenly to the dark corner she inhabited in the back of her mind. But she didn't let her guard down. The assassin was doing the mental equivalent of glaring daggers at her, and even a momentary slip by Sparrow would let the murderous woman regain control if she weren't careful.

She couldn't remember the last several hours, except for snippets: the dead body of Hayley Uvalde on the rooftop; the discovery that the King's Cross had used a drone to warn her of Wolf's intent to shoot at the stage; the desperate chase through the city; and the King's Cross agent in front of her killing Wolf and saving her, when all the woman really needed to do was wait and watch while they killed each other. Then, she could have made her escape.

"Why?" Sparrow asked the woman through a dry throat.

The enemy agent shrugged, studying Sparrow's facemask as if she might somehow pierce its veil to see the woman underneath, but said nothing.

"The drone," Sparrow croaked out the next question she desperately wanted an answer to. "Why?"

The Promethean frowned but, this time, decided to respond. "Couldn't let him do it. Didn't want a war."

"But…the president?"

"Had to die," the King's Cross agent said simply. Then she looked meaningfully at the body of Wolf next to Fox on the pavement. "And now you know why."

Despite herself, Sparrow nodded slowly, her brain still racing to process the things Wolf had said.

"What happens now?" the Promethean asked, almost casually. "You take me in? Or kill me here?" She could almost detect the hope in the other woman's voice at the last part. Sparrow knew, with no doubt, that the woman would never allow herself to be taken alive. Sparrow would win, sure. She was fresher and better armed—and all she'd have to do was let Lola back in control to end this—but she'd lose her quarry nonetheless. King's Cross agents were nasty that way, and no one on Koratas would ever get a chance to probe this woman's brain for the secrets it contained. She would kill herself first.

"Go."

It was a tossup who was more surprised by the single word. The Promethean, who had heard it, or Sparrow, who had said it.

To the other woman's credit, she didn't argue. She just walked in an arc around Sparrow, who fought a last-second and surprisingly feeble surge by Lola to take control. The enemy agent kept her distance and then stepped over the bodies of Fox and Wolf. Then, without a backward glance, she was gone.

Sparrow had never revealed her face to the other woman, keeping it hidden behind her mask, but she would never forget the King's Cross agent's features; one day, she might need to hunt her again.

SEVENTY
A NEW NAME
SPARROW

The debrief had been short and brusque. If Sparrow had harbored any hope or doubts about the Guard's involvement in the attempted assassination of Estrella Ignacio Fournier, the way Nest and the others had reacted—or rather failed to—as she'd relayed her discovery of Wolf's betrayal disabused her of those notions. They were knee-deep in it. All of them.

At least one thing had gone her way. Someone—in fact, Trina—had leaked to the press a drone photo of the fleeing King's Cross agent. With the woman's stomach laid bare through her ripped shirt, the large tattoo on it was obvious even in the overhead image. It was an instantly recognizable design, that of the Leopardo Cartel, a feared group of drug runners who operated across Koratan space. Since one of the few positive things President Ignacio Juarez had done during his tenure had been to crack down on the cartel, it didn't take the news services long to declare that it had been the Leopardos who had ordered and carried out the president's assassination. Any potential furor against the Prometheans almost instantly dissipated.

Sparrow's superiors were upset; whatever plans their former president had initiated to start a war were foiled. But without Ignacio Juarez alive to raise a fuss, they seemed content to let things lie and instead carefully watch the outcome of the election to determine who their next master would be.

But that still left them the question of what to do with their two remaining loose ends. Raven was easy; he folded to pressure and agreed not to make waves. Sparrow was more stubborn, and Nest knew her well enough to know that the young woman wouldn't simply let things lie; she would keep digging if they let her.

The senior members of the Guard recommended she be disposed of, but Nest intervened; whether out of some hope that one day Sparrow would come around or out of loyalty to an agent under her command was unclear. So, they called it a new assignment: an extended undercover infiltration of the Leeward Republic. Ostensibly, Sparrow was being sent there to gather intel on both the Republic and the Promethean Federation's southern flank and funnel it back via a series of handlers to the Confederacy.

In reality? 'Exile' was the word that readily came to mind.

They gave her eight hours to pack her things and get off the planet. Before she went, she stopped by to see the documents specialists deep in the bowels of Guard headquarters.

I hate it down here; these guys smell malo, Trina complained, as she always did visiting the documents people, but Sparrow could tell that her heart wasn't in it.

The document experts are important to the plan; they always are, Katarina tried to argue back at Trina just as languidly.

Victoria refused to even wake up and talk to the rest of them.

And Lola? Since that last attempt to seize control in the alley, the assassin had been silent. But Sparrow knew she was still there, biding her time…waiting. The woman had almost taken control permanently, and that terrified Sparrow. It also made accepting her exile a lot easier; it would be good to get far away and figure things out somewhere the rest of the Guard couldn't see.

Then, something surprising hit Sparrow just as she was reaching out to grasp and open the door to the documents office.

Where am I? a new voice asked in her mind. *What's going on?*

Sparrow paused, one hand on the door but her entire body abruptly rooted to the spot and frozen.

What is this place? the voice asked with increasing panic in its tone. It was so familiar…

Chi sei? Lola demanded with a snarl, springing forward out of her hidden corner and beginning to root around Sparrow's brain, searching for the intruder.

I'm…I'm…I don't know where I am! The new voice was practically sobbing now.

Lola, you're scaring the poor garota! Victoria interjected herself, mentally standing between the assassin and the now frantic intruder. *Querida, you're safe. Just tell us your name.*

Is that…? Trina started to ask, but Katarina shushed her.

But why is she here? Trina pressed.

Our new mission needs an intelligence officer, Katarina said, a measure of excitement in her voice. *None of us specialize in that, so Sparrow had to bring in someone new to join us.*

"Agent Sparrow, can I help you with something?" a man's voice asked. Sparrow shook herself out of her stupor and saw one of the document experts standing behind her in the hallway. She still stood in shocked silence, grasping the door handle to his domain and blocking his way back into it.

"I…uh…I need a new identity for an extended mission,"

she finally said. "Something deep enough to pass any checks thrown at it, but with no ties back to the Confederacy. Sabes?"

The man nodded thoughtfully and then indicated for her to enter the room ahead of him, which she did.

"We have several of those," he said as he walked around to sit down at a long desk covered in console screens and printers. "Blank IDs backstopped through an independent system called Kate's Hope. I'll prepare one right away; I only need a name to attach to it. Doesn't really matter which name you choose, but it should be something you remember easily. Have one in mind?"

Sparrow turned her thoughts back inward. Victoria had calmed down the newcomer now and was explaining to the girl where she was and why—at least why Katarina thought—she was there. Lola was back in hiding, her momentary reemergence foiled by, of all people, Victoria.

The new girl wasn't taking it well, nor was Sparrow. She hadn't had anyone new in there since…well, since Lola had shown up shortly after she'd joined the Guard. Before that had been Victoria, who arrived just after puberty. Katarina and Trina had been with her for as long as she could remember.

"Agent Sparrow, are you OK?" The document man's voice broke her out of her thoughts again, and she looked at him across the desk, doing her best not to show how startled she was.

"I need a name, Agent," he pressed. "Any name. If you want, I can make one up for you."

"No!" Katarina, Trina, and Victoria all cried out in unison and with such emphasis that the man shied back, and his eyes went wide.

"No," Sparrow repeated, reasserting herself and making her tone gentle. "I mean, I have a name in mind."

"And…what is it?" he asked after a moment when she didn't continue.

Sparrow took a deep breath and mentally examined the newcomer once again. Katarina was right; none of them were intelligence officers, so it made sense that they would need one for this mission. But this was the first time one of her personalities had manifested as a real person she'd known, and she wasn't sure what that meant.

"I have the name," she said again, doing her best to smile at the man.

"And?" he pressed.

She smiled again, though this time it was sincere—the first sincere smile she'd made since seeing the flashes on that rooftop and throwing herself in front of the first daughter.

"Uvalde. Hayley Uvalde."

SEVENTY-ONE
FINAL GOODBYES
NANETTE FOURNIER

Nanette looked around the bedroom one last time. Besides the furniture, none of which she could afford to ship back home to Nouveau Bourbon, she had cleared the room of any personal items, just as she'd done to Estrella's room across the hall.

Now that it was finally time to go, she found herself oddly melancholy. She may have hated her late husband and desperately wanted to be free from him, but the home on Serenidad had been hers for two decades. It was the place where she'd raised her daughter, and the times when Francisco had not been home hadn't been terrible. Sometimes, they'd even been happy.

Despite all that, she squared her shoulders resolutely and turned to leave the room, then stopped short as she cleared the doorway.

"Jonas?" she asked, seeing her husband's former adviser standing in the hall waiting for her.

"Hello, señora," the old man said with a wan smile. "I was wondering if you and I might talk before you leave the planet."

Fifteen minutes later, in a nearby sitting room, Nanette sat with mouth agape as Jonas finished an outlandish story of assassins, nations at war, and her husband's treason and complicity in the attempted murder of their own daughter.

"How? Why?" she asked, her mind reeling from all he'd told her.

Jonas looked sadder than she'd ever seen him and only shook his head. "Money, power, the usual reasons. Francisco always craved both, and that made him an easy mark for whoever outside the Confederacy wanted this war."

"But who is it, Jonas?" she pressed. "Who would *want* to kill millions of people in Koratas and Prometheus?"

The old man shook his head again. "We have no idea. Francisco was careful, and even our attempts to track the money have met with dead ends. Perhaps the Guard would have the resources to trace it back to its source, but they're hunkering down and licking their wounds after their failure both to protect your husband and...kill your daughter."

At that, Nanette felt an anger rise inside her. It was a new feeling; for two decades, she'd suppressed her bitterness at her forced marriage to Francisco. When he'd beat her, she'd tamped down her emotions so much that it often felt like he was hitting someone else, and she was only a spectator. She recognized now that even the overwhelming love she'd always felt for Estrella was muffled by her attempts to shut off all her feelings just to survive. Now, with Jonas' revelation, it was as if a shroud were removed from her eyes, and she could see and feel everything with a clarity that she'd forgotten was even possible.

She stood up, clenching her fists and looking down at the old man. "We can't let this slide, Jonas! We have to find whoever did this, and we...we must *stop* them."

The words should have surprised her. Nanette Fournier hadn't even stood up to her husband in any meaningful way in two decades. Now she was determined to stand up for a star nation that wasn't even her own? All because their enemies, whoever they were, had threatened her daughter?

For the first time since coming to her, Jonas gave her a sincere smile. "I was hoping you would say that, señora. Because I agree; so do others, in fact. But we cannot do it without your help."

Nanette nodded and sat back down, her body still trembling from the rage she felt. "Tell me what you need me to do," she said through clenched teeth.

Jonas' smile got even wider, and he leaned forward to explain his plan to her. As he spoke, the anger in Nanette's heart hardened to resolve. By the end of the conversation, he'd convinced her: she was no longer returning to her mother's star nation. No, she would stay here and save this one.

EPILOGUE

ONE MONTH LATER

Chance Fuller, better known as the Duke of Serravo, wiped the pasta sauce off his mouth and checked another number on his implant as he chewed. Farm yields in Serravo's northern hemisphere were lower than the previous year, and that had decreased exports to surrounding systems by five percentage points and done terrible things to his balance of trade. Overall GDP was down almost ten percent, and his economic advisers hadn't yet figured out a feasible plan for making up the shortfall. He'd already fired three of them to send a message to the others.

Sick of dwelling on the negative figures, he switched his implant's view to show the text of the latest commerce bill he planned to get King Charles to sponsor. On the surface, the bill seemed straightforward and even boring, a simple adjustment to certain taxes and tariffs that would make little difference to most industries. In fact, if anything, it appeared to favor smaller systems, sure to appease the very loud and growing segment of Parliament that demanded such.

Only on a far deeper review, however, one might notice the language that changed the method for measuring gross delivered product vs. waste on higher tonnage sugar freighters. It was a small, seemingly innocuous change, at least at first and even second glance, but one that would put quite a bit of money in the pockets of three of the Fringe's largest sugar cartels—which were, of course, really only one cartel with three different names. And they, showing their gratitude for the small but impactful change, would share some of that windfall with a certain shell corporation out of Denton III, which happened to be owned by a myriad of other companies that, only with supreme effort, could be traced back to Chance Fuller III, Duke of Serravo.

He smiled at the thought of the money to come. Duke Fuller had no doubt that good old King Charles wouldn't even question the bill presented to him by his closest adviser and dear, dear cousin. He so seldom questioned *anything* Chance pushed him to do these days. He'd been very impressionable indeed, ever since his son's diagnosis.

Of course, that didn't mean things had all gone the way Fuller wanted them to, and he frowned as he took another bite of dinner. Something had happened with the King's Cross agent he'd convinced Charles to send to Koratas. The woman had failed her mission to kill the stupid Fournier tramp and her idiot daughter. She hadn't even gotten herself captured as he and Ignacio Juarez had hoped. And despite the official story of some drug cartel killing Ignacio Juarez, Fuller had little doubt it had been the same King's Cross agent who had actually pulled the trigger.

The supposedly loyal and always effective King's Cross had faltered and even betrayed them, dealing a severe blow to Duke Fuller's meticulously laid plans. With that failure, his own aspirations had almost crumbled.

Still, he was confident. So long as Charles listened to him and only him, there was still a very real chance he could get the war started again. He just needed to…

A noise in the hall outside his private dining room interrupted his train of thought. It was a dull thud, like something heavy but soft had fallen.

"Antoní?" he called through the closed door.

His steward did not respond, and he frowned. If the man were sitting down on the job again, he would lose that job as quickly as Chance could catch him in the act…maybe quicker, regardless. He called the man's name again, but there was no reply.

Sighing, Fuller levered himself out of his seat and padded across the thick carpet in his dinner slippers to the door, pushing it open and peering out into the hall.

Nothing. No sign of Antoní or anything that could have fallen. Strange…

He closed the door and turned back to the table but stopped short as he saw there was a woman sitting in his seat!

"Guards!" he screamed as he first caught a glimpse of her, but something was off, and his voice sounded muffled in the large dining room, not even echoing off the high domed ceiling as it usually did. It was almost like he was screaming underwater.

Panic seized him, and he turned to rush back to the door but stopped short again when the hilt of a knife suddenly appeared lodged in the heavy wood in front of him, still quivering from its fast flight through the air to stick in that spot.

"Next one goes in your back if you don't take a seat, now," the woman said behind him, almost conversationally, though her own voice was just as muffled as his.

He almost called her bluff, but the sight of the wicked blade embedded in the door was enough to convince him she meant the threat and could follow through on it. He turned slowly and moved back toward the table, studying her as he approached.

His first impression was that she was young and pretty,

with fiery red shoulder-length hair, striking features, and a freckled complexion under startling green eyes. But when he took in the expression on her face, all thoughts of her being either pretty or young fled. Chance Fuller himself was not a killer—at least not in person—but he'd employed enough of them over the years to recognize the signs. This was a dangerous woman, and for some reason, she was very ticked off at *him*.

"What do you want?" he demanded nonetheless as he slowly sat in the seat she indicated, frowning to see her helping herself to the remains of his dinner.

She chewed for a few seconds, ignoring him as if he hadn't spoken at all, though he got the distinct impression that she was still watching him closely enough that even a twitch on his part would result in his untimely death. So, he waited her out.

Finally, swallowing her latest bite, she sat back in the seat she'd stolen from him and regarded him with a hard gaze. He tried to match it, to stare back at her with all of the indignation of a ruler of three systems and a cousin to the King of over a hundred, but he found himself involuntarily breaking eye contact first. Even then, she still said nothing but kept glaring at him.

"What do you want?" he asked again, unable to bear the silent scrutiny any longer. This time, his voice cracked, audible even through the sound-dampening field she'd somehow employed to cover this room.

"Actually, the question is, what do *you* want?" she said almost casually.

He looked back up at her, failing to keep the incredulity off his face. "What? What do you mean?" He was frantically trying to call his security team on his implant but kept getting a connection error. In addition to the sound dampening, she was also jamming his comms.

"You're the third, possibly even the second most powerful person in the Federation these days." Her semi-muffled voice was still infuriatingly casual. "You ought to be used to telling people what you want, even when they don't ask. So tell me, Duke, what do you want?"

"My guards will be here any second!" he sputtered, ignoring her nonsensical query. "If you leave now, you might—"

"Tsk, tsk, tsk," she interrupted him with a slow shake of her head. "Perhaps I'll make the question simpler. You recently convinced King Charles to send a member of the Order of the King's Cross to Koratas to assassinate the first lady and first daughter there. That much I know, without a doubt. But I want to know *why* you did it."

Chance's anger and indignation up to this point were suddenly replaced by a cold knot in his stomach. His eyes went wide, and he gaped at the woman, opening his mouth to automatically deny the claim, but she beat him to it.

"Don't bother denying it," she said with a grim smile. "I've seen the messages between you and Ignacio Juarez. And I know it was you who recommended the assassination and ultimately convinced Charles to order it. And I know that it *wasn't* for the reasons you told him. So, I did some digging, and do you know what I found?"

Chance couldn't help it; he shook his head dumbly.

She raised her eyebrows at him and continued. "I found the two billion-credit *consulting* fee paid to one of your cleverly hidden shell companies by the Noragan Consortium. I wondered what kind of consulting you did for them that paid two *billion* credits. Of course, that was before I realized that Noragan was a shell company owned by Telegen Holdings, which in turn was owned by… Why don't I just cut to the end of the story? Of course, you know already that Noragan and Telegen are ultimately owned by NSX Arms."

She paused, eyeing him speculatively, perhaps to see if he would react or respond. He didn't say anything, but he knew instantly that he hadn't schooled his expression well enough to hide his surprise and guilt.

The woman in black smiled broadly, this time as if he'd just given her all the confession she needed, but the smile disappeared quickly as she leaned across the corner of the table toward him and started idly flipping a small knife in one hand.

"Tell me, Duke," she growled, her anger coming through even with her voice muffled, "did you at least pretend that you weren't helping NSX start a war purely so they could profit from selling arms to both sides? Did you at least lie to yourself about why they wanted the Prometheans to commit an act of war against Koratas? Or did you simply accept the money *knowing* and not caring that it would result in millions or even billions dying in a never-ending war?"

She leaned back and kept talking, not giving him time to respond. "Me? I'm an optimist…well, sort of. I prefer to think that you were simply stupid rather than as malicious as *knowing* would make you. Which is why I'm here to offer you a deal."

The redheaded woman paused now, her gaze turning harder than before. Finally, Chance Fuller found his voice.

"You're the one Charles sent to do it! You disobeyed your orders. He's already commanded the rest of the Order to hunt you down and kill you!" He tried to imbue his voice with righteous anger, but even in the muffled room, he knew it sounded more desperate than anything.

To his surprise, she smiled again. "Well, I suppose you're not as dumb as I hoped you'd be. Which is why you're going to share with me, here and now, every file—every shred of detail—about your dealings with NSX. Are. We. Clear?" She bit off the last three words, and the knife she'd been idly flipping in her hand suddenly spun up into her closed and outstretched fist, pointed right at his left eye from less than four centimeters away.

Chance flinched and felt a warmth in his pants and an overpowering sense of helplessness and embarrassment as his bladder released. The woman showed no reaction other than to wrinkle her nose at the smell. Her eyes stayed steady and unblinking, though he only saw her as a blurred image as both his eyes attempted to focus on the point of the knife in front of his face. But he could *feel* her stare, boring into him so hard he felt like she could already read *everything* she wanted from his implant, even though that was impossible.

"You're going to kill me anyway," he stammered. "But NSX will come after my family, too, if I tell you anything."

Slowly, she shook her head. "No. They won't."

"How can you be so sure?" he demanded.

She smiled again, showing her teeth and making him feel like he might pee himself again. "Because I'm going after *them* next."

"That's madness," he protested despite himself. "They're an Inner Rim company. Their tech is light years beyond ours; they'll see you coming from a hundred parsecs away! Even the King's Cross can't go up against them."

Her smile disappeared, and her next words came in a snarl. "Duke Fuller, I'm afraid you severely underestimate the King's Cross. More importantly, you underestimate *me*. Because let me be crystal clear. I'm the King's Cross agent who is currently being hunted by *every* other member of my order, and I still made it here to your stronghold and your inner sanctum and came within centimeters of killing you. And I want you to think very carefully about what will happen to you if you don't give me what I want. NSX may kill you later, but I will kill you *now* in the most unimaginable way possible."

He nodded and gulped, surrendering and pinging all the files on NSX and his communications with them to her implant. Chance didn't even consider holding anything back, afraid that she'd know and follow through on her threat.

Once the transfer was done, she disappeared almost just as suddenly as she'd appeared. He cried out for his guards, but a thorough search of the palace and the surrounding city turned up nothing.

The former King's Cross agent had escaped and, if her words to him were to be believed, was now en route to the Inner Rim, hundreds of light years away, to face down a corporation of killers even deadlier than herself.

Given that both would kill him if given the chance, Fuller couldn't decide who he was rooting for in the upcoming fight but was certain that blood would soon be shed in violent fashion. All that was left to be seen was whether or not he and his entire star nation survived the battle to come.

THE END OF BOOK TWO

The adventures of Hayley Uvalde and Nanette Fournier continue in *The Worst Traitors in the Confederacy,* book six of *Dumb Luck and Dead Heroes.*

Don't ever miss a new release!

Sign up now for Skyler's newsletter and get access to new release updates, free content, and great deals.

Just go to www.skylerramirez.com/join-the-club

BOOKS BY SKYLER RAMIREZ

DUMB LUCK AND DEAD HEROES

The Worst Ship in the Fleet

The Worst Spies in the Sector

The Worst Pirate Hunters in the Fringe

The Worst Rescuers in the Republic

The Worst Detectives in the Federation

The Worst Traitors in the Confederacy

The Worst Fugitives in the Star Nation

The Worst Mercenaries in the Border Systems

The Worst Admiral in the Star Cluster (Coming Soon)

A STAR NATION IN PERIL

Set in the same universe as Dumb Luck and Dead Heroes

Rogue Agent

Suicide Mission

Assassin's Flight

THE GALAXY'S WORST MERCENARIES

Set in the same universe as Dumb Luck and Dead Heroes

The Kaelen Extraction: A Billy Firebrand Adventure (Coming Soon)

THE BRAD MENDOZA CHRONICLES

Short stories in the same universe as Dumb Luck and Dead Heroes

Saving the Academy

Battle for Poe

Siege of Jalisco

Death Station

Bells and Bullets

THE FOUR WORLDS

The Four Worlds: The Truth

The Four Worlds: Subversion

The Four Worlds: Wrath of Mars

Ascension (Working Title; Coming 2026)

Revolution: A Four Worlds Story

ANTHOLOGIES

AI Apocalypse: A Collection of Science Fiction Stories (with Jonathan Yanez, Andrew Moriarty, Anthony J Melchiorri, and Stephen Gay)

STANDALONE SHORT STORIES

Serena

ABOUT THE AUTHOR

I just love writing. My goal is to write books that my readers enjoy and that celebrate everyday imperfect heroes. I want to show that everyone, no matter how life has dealt with them or how they've dealt with life, deserves a second chance and can go on to do amazing things. Just look at Brad and Jessica in Dumb Luck and Dead Heroes or Jinny Ambrosa and Tyrus Tyne in The Four Worlds.

It's important to me that everyone be able to read my books, including my teenage children, so I purposefully leave out any swearing or graphic scenes, though I don't shy away from serious topics. In this, I follow a tradition set by many (far better) writers before me, most notably in my life, Louis L'Amour.

As for the personal side, I live in Texas with my wife and four children (and often a revolving door of exchange students), and I work for a major tech company in my spare time. But writing is my passion, and I often toil into the early hours of morning, especially on the weekends, and it's all worth it when I see people enjoy my books.

Thanks for reading!

Skyler Ramirez

amazon.com/author/Skyler-Ramirez
facebook.com/skylerramirezauthor
instagram.com/skyler.ramirez.author
tiktok.com/@skylerramirez_author

Printed in Dunstable, United Kingdom

72863931R00141